ALSO BY PAOLO MAURENSIG

The Lüneburg Variation

Canone Inverso

THEORY OF SHADOWS

PAOLO MAURENSIG

THEORY OF SHADOWS

TRANSLATED FROM THE ITALIAN BY ANNE MILANO APPEL

NEW YORK

FARRAR, STRAUS AND GIROUX ■

Farrar, Straus and Giroux
175 Varick Street, New York 10014

Copyright © 2015 by Adelphi Edizioni S.p.A.
Translation copyright © 2018 by Anne Milano Appel
All rights reserved
Printed in the United States of America
Originally published in Italian in 2015 by Adelphi Edizioni, Italy, as
  Teoria delle ombre
English translation published in the United States by Farrar, Straus
  and Giroux
First American edition, 2018

Library of Congress Cataloging-in-Publication Data
Names: Maurensig, Paolo, 1943– author. | Appel, Anne Milano,
  translator.
Title: Theory of shadows / Paolo Maurensig ; translated from the
  Italian by Anne Milano Appel.
Other titles: Teoria delle ombre. English
Description: First American edition. | New York : Farrar, Straus and
  Giroux, 2018. | "Originally published in Italian in 2015 by Adelphi
  Edizioni, Italy, as Teoria delle ombre" — Verso title page. | Novel
  inspired by the death of Alexander Alekhine (1892–1946), Russian
  chess player, naturalized French citizen.
Identifiers: LCCN 2017028943| ISBN 9780374273804 (hardcover) |
  ISBN 9780374715915 (ebook)
Subjects: LCSH: Alekhine, Alexander, 1892–1946—Fiction. |
  GSAFD: Biographical fiction.
Classification: LCC PQ4873.A8947 T46513 2018 |
  DDC 853/.914—dc23
LC record available at https://lccn.loc.gov/2017028943

Designed by Richard Oriolo

Our books may be purchased in bulk for promotional, educational, or
business use. Please contact your local bookseller or the Macmillan
Corporate and Premium Sales Department at 1-800-221-7945, extension
5442, or by e-mail at MacmillanSpecialMarkets@macmillan.com.

www.fsgbooks.com
www.twitter.com/fsgbooks • www.facebook.com/fsgbooks

10 9 8 7 6 5 4 3 2 1

If Alekhine had been a Jew-hating Nazi scientist, inventor of weapons of extermination and therefore protected by those in power, then that intellectual rabble would have cravenly held its breath. Instead, the victim had to drain the bitter cup to the last drop . . . Even the supreme act of his death was vulgarly besmirched. And we cowards stifled our feelings, remaining silent. Because the only virtue that fraternally unites us all, whites and blacks, Jews and Christians, is cowardice.

—Esteban Canal

CONTENTS

PROLOGUE

ONCE AGAIN I wake up in the dead of night, smothered by the late-August heat, and, finding myself lying in a bed at this modest hotel in Estoril, I am overcome by anxiety. The question that for years has been haunting me is only amplified in the nocturnal solitude and silence, until it becomes deafening. Will I finally be able to find an answer?

It all started with my inveterate passion for chess. I have never played in a qualifying tournament, or achieved standing in the official ranking; indeed, I consider myself an enthusiastic amateur. Still, say what you like, but even a café player can draw great satisfaction from the game. After all, when you are competing with opponents of your own caliber, the excitement you feel is not very different from that experienced by the champions. There is also the pleasure of research, of studying the games played by the great masters of the past, and even of discovering how tormented their lives must have been, precisely because of their absolute devotion to the formidable idol that is chess. Lives that often ended tragically.

I was born in Venezuela and spent my childhood in Caracas. My father died when I was only five. My mother then went to work as a governess in a family of Italians who had made a fortune in the catering business. She was well liked, and was herself very attached to them, so when they decided to return to Italy, we moved, too, settling in the capital.

Since my intention is to talk about someone else's life, however, I shouldn't dwell on my own, which up until the age of fifty was spent in precious mediocrity. When I suddenly decided to write a novel, I did so not out of a desire to deliver myself from a gray existence, but solely because I was driven by an obsession: to discover the cause of a man's death, which took place sixty-six years ago. That man is Aleksandr Aleksandrovich Alekhin, better known as Alexandre Alekhine, and if I somehow learned to play chess at a level that is, to me, satisfactory, I owe it all to him. I owe it to the study of his unparalleled games and the comments he made, in a clear, comprehensible way, concerning the various phases of his game and the strategies applied during the course of every single match. He has been my role model for many years now, my tutelary deity.

Only recently, though, did I begin looking into his past, and it was from there that the idea of writing a novel sprang. Not so much about his life, actually, as about the final days leading up to his as yet unexplained death. To do that, I had to adopt the garb of an investigator determined to reopen the case of a crime long since filed away unsolved. I went to Lisbon, and I visited all the chess clubs, starting with the Turf Club, along the very fashionable Rua Garrett, down to

4

the last smoke-filled dive in Estoril; there I made several contacts, passing myself off as a journalist interested in writing an article on Alekhine's life.

My knowledge of Portuguese—which was my mother's language—was of great help to me in communicating with the locals. Still, according to what I've been able to learn so far, word is that there's only one man who can give me any fresh information on the events in question. His name is Rui Nascimento. Chess player, problemist, musician, and poet, he is a very popular figure in Lisbon. Unfortunately, he has been admitted to the hospital, dying. And it's not surprising, seeing that he's reached the enviable age of ninety-eight. Still, I decided to visit him anyway. I thought that perhaps I might get a chance to speak with one of his family members. Instead, I didn't even have the nerve to cross the threshold of his room. His bed was next to a curtained window through which a milky light seeped in. Around him, several women dressed in black were absorbed in prayer. I only managed to get a glimpse of his aquiline profile, rendered more hooked by his hollow cheeks: a face already reduced to a funerary mask.

Thus, no new information has been added to what I've already turned up through my research. In the more than sixty years that have passed since the time of Alekhine's death, with the advent of the Internet, the number of hypotheses—many of which I would not care to share—has multiplied beyond belief. There remain, however, a number of facts that have been certified and documented.

■

ON THE MORNING of Sunday, March 24, 1946, Alexandre Alekhine, world chess champion, was found lifeless in his room at the Hotel do Parque, in Estoril. It was the waiter assigned to bring him breakfast who sounded the alarm. Having entered with the food trolley, he saw the master sitting in his usual armchair; with his eyes closed and his head tilted back, he appeared to be asleep. Instead of his smoking jacket, he was wearing an overcoat; his left arm hung limply at his side, and his fingers were clutching a piece of meat.

News of his death, attributed to a heart attack, was soon announced by a Portuguese radio station. The following day, the *Daily Mail* wrote that Alekhine had taken his own life after suffering a huge loss at the casino. The death certificate was written up the same day by Dr. Antonio Jacinto Ferreira, who, three days later, was also present at the autopsy performed by Dr. Asdrúbal d'Aguiar. It was reported that a piece of meat had occluded his airway, asphyxiating him. Moreover, it was revealed that the deceased suffered from chronic gastritis, duodenitis, and atherosclerosis. Strangely, no mention was made of the condition of either his heart or his liver, though Alekhine's problems with alcohol were known to all.

Luís Lupi—stepfather of Francisco Lupi, chess champion of Portugal and a friend of Alekhine—was among the first to rush over and take a few photographs. Two of the four snapshots quickly traveled around the world, published in hundreds of magazines and newspapers.

These same photographs, disclosed with the intent of confirming that the master had expired peacefully, produced the opposite result, raising numerous doubts concerning the official version. If you compare the two snapshots, which were taken from different angles, certain objects in fact appear to have been shifted slightly; this fueled misgivings that the scene had been carefully prepared in order to convince readers and chess fans that the world champion had died of natural causes (and consequently to put to rest even the slightest suspicion of a violent death). Although Alekhine had been accused of collaborating with the Nazis, it was a source of pride for Portugal to host the world chess champion; his sudden death was therefore a matter of grave embarrassment for the government. The general impression was that the authorities were doing everything possible to play down the incident. This task was assigned to the PIDE (Polícia Internacional e de Defesa do Estado), which at that time controlled all aspects of Portuguese life with an iron fist: it imposed a rigorous censorship on newspapers and radio stations, and quickly filed away the case, without launching any further investigations.

Nevertheless, some spoke up. The first was Artur Portela, a journalist in open conflict with the Salazar regime. Even though he was considered a subversive and was constantly under the scrutiny of the secret police, Portela was untouchable. He was renowned throughout Europe for his interviews with great statesmen—among them Generalissimo Franco and Winston Churchill—and King George VI of England had recently conferred on him the Order of Liberty.

In an article published on April 15 in *Diário de Lisboa*, entitled "O segredo do Quarto 43: A morte misteriosa de Alexandre Alekhine" ("The Secret of Room 43: The Mysterious Death of Alexandre Alekhine"), he examined the various inconsistencies that appeared when he attempted to reconstruct the events of that fateful morning. To begin with, he pointed out that news of Alekhine's death had spread well before the waiter had discovered the lifeless body. Referring to the published photos, he then wondered why the master, merely to sit at his own table, had put on a heavy coat instead of a smoking jacket—the Portuguese spring was already quite warm.

Artur Portela was also the first to air the theory of homicide, suggesting the involvement of agents of the Kremlin. With due prudence, however, he ruled out any complicity on the part of Salazar's secret police. All the same, his conjectures were ridiculed, attributed to a writer's fertile imagination. Very soon, moreover, the international press, at first respectful, became ruthless, choosing to focus on the ambiguous figure of the champion, his excesses, bringing to light details of his life that were not very edifying, such as his habit of eating meat with his hands and drinking nothing short of three pints of cognac every day. According to a statement by Grandmaster Hans Kmoch, Alekhine and his last wife, Grace Wishaar, traveled around the world with, in addition to a number of cats, a whole trunk filled with liquor bottles: a portable stash.

Numerous testimonies were gathered—some not very reliable—from those who claimed to have known him closely, and they, too, helped to create a very ambivalent portrait of the man.

Nor was the possibility of suicide ruled out.

That he had self-destructive tendencies was confirmed by the chess player Edmond Lancel, who reported encountering Alekhine—in 1922, on his birthday, in Aix-la-Chapelle—at three in the morning, as he was wandering through the deserted lobby of the Grand Hotel Corneliusbad. He thought Alekhine was ill, and when he approached to help him, the master fell unconscious at his feet, bleeding profusely from a wound in the abdomen that (it was later discovered) he had inflicted on himself with a kitchen knife. Alekhine was promptly rushed to the hospital. When he was discharged, after a week, the doctors recommended complete rest, but a few days later he was already participating in a tournament. The story behind that injury remained obscure; people preferred to attribute it to a general state of extreme fatigue.

Reuben Fine, a psychoanalyst and a candidate for the world chess title (he was the first to object strenuously to Alekhine's participation in the London tournament of 1946), would subsequently sketch a disturbing psychological portrait of the master, describing him as "the sadist of the chess world" and going so far as to speculate that even at an early age he had suffered from impotence, likely caused by alcoholism. But it was chiefly based on Alekhine's political positions that the attacks on him multiplied. There were those who saw him as an opportunist, a man without ideals, ready to change his stripes at any moment; he was said to be a spy, a double agent, a traitor. Some claimed that he had been involved with the famous cryptographic machine called Enigma, and that he had first worked as a British intelligence agent before then going over to the enemy; others contended that, having been enlisted in a British secret-service "ghost cell" headed by Ian Fleming, and not officially recognized by the High Command, he had lost all contact with his recruiters, finding it impossible to clarify his position.

But the worst infamy that was attributed to him, the indelible stain that Alekhine carried with him during the final years of his life, was his friendship with Reichsminister Hans Frank, governor of Poland. At the end of the war, he was left with few friends: to the French he was a collaborator, to the Soviets a traitor; even the White Russians who had settled in Europe would not forgive him for having worked, during the Revolution, for the ministry tasked with expropriating the assets of emigrants.

As a result, he certainly wasn't lacking in enemies, but if—as I believe—Alekhine was murdered, what I'm still missing is a plausible motive. And I know that you cannot write a story centered on a crime without unmasking the killer at the end.

■

THOUGH I CAME here to find a conceivable ending to my novel, it seems increasingly likely that I will leave without having accomplished anything. I spoke to the old people in the area. I deluded myself that everyone would remember something about Alekhine, but to the majority of them that name means absolutely nothing. Only one man, hearing me say it, gave an imperceptible start, as though the gear tooth of a cogwheel had clicked into place in his memory's mechanism.

"*Ah, sim, o campeão mundial de xadrez*"—"Oh yes, the world chess champion."

THEN, TOO, I can't help finding myself weighed down by the sense of distance one feels when noting the changes that have taken place over the years. Now, faced with cold reality, the impeccable mental structure that I'd built in narrating Alekhine's story is crumbling like a sand castle. If you compare Estoril as it is now with postcards from the first postwar period—printed in black and white, or at most touched up with a few strokes of color—you realize how different it must have appeared at that time: the wild coast, mostly covered by low, shrubby thicket, is merely a remote memory, and the charming hotel where Alekhine met his death no longer exists, having been demolished in the 1970s in favor of a modern structure only vaguely reminiscent of the earlier one. This new Hotel do Parque is one of the most celebrated hotels in the vicinity, and the beach, which at that time was rarely frequented by bathers, becomes in summer a carnival of multicolored umbrellas, with bathing establishments stretching as far as the eye can see.

Had I shortened my stay by a few days, I would have been able to afford the luxury of staying at the Hotel do Parque myself—indeed, I might even have been able to satisfy my desire to occupy Room 43, which, in the master's memory, still bears a doorplate engraved with his name—but I was afraid that, confronted with reality, the setting that I had already depicted in my pages might fade altogether. Only once did I venture to set foot in the lobby, but I left almost immediately. Seeing the bar, its modern design, as icy as a gelato parlor, was enough to make my stomach tighten. Everything was so fake, so contrived. Even that doorplate makes me smile. I couldn't begin to guess whose idea it was to put it there, and though I appreciate the thought, it reminds me too much of a bunch of withered flowers laid at the foot of a tree where some unfortunate drove off the road and lost his life.

So I chose a different hotel, small, not too far away. I walk to the shore in the early mornings, when there are still only a few people out. It's not long before the beach gets crowded, but there's one stretch of rocky coast that remains untouched by this mass incursion of bathers—the one that leads to the lighthouse, along the same narrow path I assume Alekhine chose for his own solitary walks. Following the trail, I like to think that I'm retracing his footsteps. Every so often I stop in some sheltered cleft among the rocks to reread the pages of the manuscript that I always carry with me, and let my mind transport me back to that far-off spring of 1946.

THEORY OF SHADOWS

I.

FROM HIS ROOM on the first floor he came down to the still-deserted lobby—deserted as it had been the day before, the week before, the month before . . . Every morning, he hoped to see a row of suitcases by the entrance, ready to be transferred to various rooms by the porter; perhaps a little family seated on the sofa, busy chatting and browsing through leaflets and brochures. But he was disappointed once more. Nothing had changed.

He crossed the spacious lobby, heading quickly for the exit, uncomfortable with the idea that the entire apparatus of the hotel was for him alone. He had not yet grown accustomed to being the hotel's only guest. Often, despite the staff's extreme courtesy toward him, he had the painful feeling that he was in their way, that they were all just waiting for him to go, so they could finally shut down. For the moment, however, it was not possible for him to leave that place.

From the floor attendant to the young man assigned to room service, everyone called him "Dr. Alexandre"—no one tried to pronounce his full name and surname, combined with its lofty-sounding patronymic. The clerk at the reception desk, who had recorded his data, confirmed that he had been born in Moscow but was traveling with a French passport. And everyone followed his movements with open curiosity as well as a trace of suspicion.

He had been there for over a month now, and rumors about his habits were beginning to circulate among the hotel staff. The imposing figure and piercing eyes alone would have been enough to inspire awe; furthermore, he had a sharp, commanding voice, and although when requesting service he always addressed the staff with a courtesy bordering on affectation, his way of enunciating his words precisely, almost spelling them out, gave the impression that he was issuing a peremptory order, expecting not to have to repeat it.

The person who noticed this first was the chef, or, rather, the waiter instructed to deliver Alekhine's message to him. When he had served him fish for the first time, the chef was told that the master hated any type of sea creature and was asked to cook him nothing but meat, preferably rare. Meat and sweets. And wine—red wine, of course. The chambermaid also had stories to tell: for days and days, in fact, she often found his bed untouched, as if Dr. Alexandre were spending entire nights without once lying down; and one day, when she accidentally entered without knocking, she had caught him sitting in his armchair, in front of a chessboard, engaged in avidly devouring some raw meat, bringing it to his mouth with his bare hands. None of the staff knew exactly who he was and what he was doing there, but everyone was quick to offer fanciful theories: for some he was a Russian spy, for others a Nazi in hiding.

Every morning, before lunch, Aleksandr Aleksandrovich Alekhin—this was the name that no one could pronounce—allowed himself a walk to the lighthouse. Along the coast, stretches of beach alternated with low rocky ridges. That day, the wind coming from the Atlantic was blowing hard, and the frequent heavy storms of the previous days had deposited mounds of seaweed ashore, along with fragments of shells and jellyfish reduced to wobbly masses of iridescent gelatin. The beach club was closed, and the so-called solarium—a wooden platform on stilts that in summer, judging by the postcards for sale at the hotel's reception desk, was packed with strapping young men and pretty girls in bathing suits—seemed in the winter light like the frail skeleton of an antediluvian animal, its long legs sunk in the sand. The Hotel do Parque, where he was staying, towered above. Along the trail leading to the promontory where the lighthouse stood, the hotel's baroque façade, covered with dazzling *azulejos*, continued to run alongside him, the way the moon appears to keep pace with us when it's low on the horizon; only from the farthest point was he able to see part of the building's inland side, the one facing the park, dense with maritime pines and tamarisk.

The beginning of spring was not far off, but swimming season would not begin before May; yet the hotel stayed open. In the dining room, tables and chairs were stacked along a wall; all his meals were served to him in his room. This room, marked by a brass plate reading number 43, was spacious enough, and had a large balcony overlooking the ocean: a magnificent view for anyone, though not for him, who viewed that infinite expanse of water as the very image of the unknown. Often, to ascertain whether there might be anyone else staying in that hermitage, he would walk from one end of his floor to the other, passing a succession of doors, all closed, all identical except for the numbers on their brass plates; sometimes he listened in front of one door or another, but he never heard the slightest sound. He'd also climbed to the upper floors, but there, too, he found doors and more doors, and not a single voice could be heard filtering out from them.

Though reduced in number, the staff were very efficient, and the chef in the kitchen was at his complete disposal. Maybe, he told himself, the hotel would soon fill with people—a conference, a seminar, or something like that. It had been a month since he'd exchanged a word with anyone, except for a few remarks with Manuel, the young man who served him his meals in his room. Time went by in a succession of long periods of sleeping and wakefulness. Day and night blurred, and the loneliness was now becoming unbearable.

The last doctor who had examined him had made an inauspicious diagnosis. The man had been explicit: his liver was in serious condition, he was suffering from acute duodenitis, and, besides that, he was beginning to show signs of angina. If he did not stop drinking excessively and smoking forty cigarettes a day, he would not live long.

"How long do I have?"

"A year at most."

"And if I stop?"

"A few more."

"Then maybe it's not worth it," he'd replied, laughing—though there was precious little that was amusing about the thought of death. In fact, fear of dying was always lurking in him, and no matter how hard he tried to bury it in the depths of his consciousness, it would crop up suddenly, usually at night, when, tormented by insomnia, he paced back and forth for hours in his room.

Eventually, however, when he was nearly broke, he was forced to stop drinking, and settle for the single bottle of Alentejo that was served with his meals.

◼

SOMETIMES HE THOUGHT about how he had come to be there, in Estoril, that last windy strip of Europe, the sole guest in a hotel open off-season. He still found it hard to believe that, at a time when everything had appeared on the verge of falling to pieces, an unexpected meeting had set him back on his feet. Almost like a sign from Providence.

Only a month earlier, in fact, he had been in Lisbon, but the management of the hotel where he was staying had literally kicked him out, confiscating his luggage until he had taken steps to settle the tab. That evening, he had wandered through the city, wondering where he would spend the night. He had only a few bills in his pocket: just enough to get a bite to eat along with a mug of beer. He had walked to the Ás de Ouros, a bar that stayed open until dawn. It was barely nine, and the place was still half empty. In the center of the room, a pair of elderly dancers shuffled around to the music of an accordion, while a few people were playing cards at some nearby tables, and there was even an area reserved for chess, though it was deserted. So he sat down in that corner and, after arranging the pieces on a board, began moving them distractedly, waiting for someone to come along and challenge him; since even chess was never played without a small wager, there was a chance he might earn an extra drink or two. He would certainly not take advantage of his skills, however, and would grant the opponent du jour a suitable advantage, as he always did.

He did not have to wait long. Someone came forward: a middle-aged man, ordinary-looking, modestly dressed; one would have said he was a sales representative for some insurance company, or else a city official.

"*Eu posso ter a honra de jogar um jogo?*"

The stranger spoke Portuguese correctly, though marked by an accent that suggested it was not his native language.

"*De boa vontade.*"

The pieces were placed back on their starting squares. The man sat down heavily in front of Alekhine, carefully arranging the flaps of the overcoat he still had on. Then he proposed: "A beer?"

"For a beer," Alekhine agreed. "But before we begin, I must warn you that I am unbeatable."

The other man smiled, skeptical. "Really?"

"I therefore feel obliged to give you an advantage."

"Which would be?"

"A Knight, a Bishop . . . even a Rook, if you like."

"No, no, if I have to lose, I prefer to do so on equal terms."

"As you wish. I warned you."

The man did not seem too concerned. The toss was favorable to him; he was White. From the very first moves it was clear that he was not exactly a novice, but after a flawless opening, he suddenly lifted his King from its square and, as a sign of surrender, laid the piece on its side in the middle of the board. The gesture was irritating to Alekhine, even downright offensive.

"What does that mean? Why do you want to give up? Your position was still a solid one."

The stranger laughed. "But my solid position would certainly not have lasted much longer against the world champion."

At that point the man, after apologizing for his little deception, introduced himself by the name of Spitzler. He said he was a government official and that he had been specifically assigned to track Alekhine down. He informed the champion that a match for the world title had already been arranged: the challenger was a Russian, whose name, however, was still not known. Soon the news would appear in the international press. He then assured Alekhine of having settled his hotel bill, and lastly handed him an envelope that contained money, along with the address of the Hotel do Parque, in Estoril, where he could stay with all expenses paid. He would hear from Spitzler again very soon.

"To whom do I owe all this?"

"You still have friends," the man said, and left.

II.

THE ENCOUNTER HAD restored Alekhine's self-confidence. He was still the world chess champion, and his pride in the title that he'd held almost uninterruptedly for more than eighteen years had been rekindled in him like a flame. He still held a valid international safe-conduct, a status that precluded any action against him. At first, being able to stay in a luxury hotel, waited on hand and foot, had seemed like a fitting recognition of his merit; but after he'd spent a few weeks waiting to hear from that Spitzler, his stay had become increasingly troubling. He felt cut off from the world. No other papers besides the *Diário de Lisboa* could be found in the lobby, and the only other outside contact was a radio he kept on his nightstand. Sometimes he managed to tune in to some crackly foreign station. Sequestered in that hotel, he felt like a bird imprisoned in a huge aviary: big enough to make him think he was free, but still holding him captive in its netting.

Participation in the London tournament, which would have been a good opportunity to earn some money, had been denied him, and now he was once again short on cash. He only had a few escudos left in his pocket: the sum given to him by the man he'd met in Lisbon had, as usual, been squandered in a couple of weeks. His indifference to the value of money definitely came from his father, who, before being stopped by the family, had burned through much of the estate, going so far as to lose two million rubles in gold at the Monte Carlo Casino in a single night.

Recently, Alekhine had written to his fourth wife, Grace Wishaar, who was handling some family property in Saint-Aubin-le-Cauf, in Upper Normandy. Although they were about to divorce, she would never have refused him financial assistance. He had also phoned Francisco Lupi, Portugal's champion and an old friend of his, asking to write a few articles for Lupi's magazine, just to earn some cigarette money, but so far he had not received a reply. All he could do was wait.

Every morning, he followed the same routine: breakfast at nine, a few hours at the chessboard, then the walk to the lighthouse; after that, around noon, he returned to his room and waited for the server to bring him his lunch, accompanied by a bottle of Alentejo.

That day, as he climbed the stairs leading from the beach to the hotel, he was forced to stop, overcome by a dull ache in his chest, a pain that he experienced whenever he faced an ascent. He had to wait a few minutes to be able to continue up. By the time he reached the hotel, the pain had subsided; eventually, it disappeared altogether. As he always did when he returned from his walk, he stopped by the reception desk in the hope that there might be a message for him, but this time, as all the others, the clerk's pitying expression was all too eloquent.

Right after eating, he lay on his bed, fully clothed, covering himself with his overcoat, and sank quickly into a soothing sleep, so different from the variety he endured at night, from which he often woke gripped by a terrible anxiety. This afternoon slumber was peaceful: in his dreams he met persons, living or long dead, who had departed with some business left unfinished, and with whom he enjoyed endless discussions. Everything in these dreams happened in a logical, coherent way: the scene remained unchanged, everything firmly in its place, and nothing bizarre or terrifying occurred, as it did in his nocturnal nightmares. Though he often found himself talking to deceased individuals in those afternoon dreams—people whose funerals he had surely attended years earlier—everything seemed very credible to him: all barriers between life and death, between past and present, stood revealed as insubstantial. Sometimes he could observe himself wondering whether these dreams were dreams at all. Doubt would only arise from some dissonant detail: someone, for example, who had never served in the military but was wearing the impeccable uniform of a tsarist captain of the guard; or one who in life had been a rigorous teetotaler but here was downing a pint of beer. Alekhine had found that, the stronger the wind blew outside, the more vivid his visions became.

That afternoon, his mother appeared to him, seated beside him in the spacious living room of the house where he had spent his youth, in Moscow. The large window that overlooked the Arbat was embroidered by winter frost. Tsar Nicholas II stood in the doorway, waiting to come in to confer a very high honor on Alekhine. Behind the tsar, the minister of culture held in his hands a blue vase of the finest Sèvres porcelain, adorned with the imperial eagle. In the dream, Alekhine knew that the tsar himself would present the vase to him in recognition of victories achieved. Nevertheless, his mother hugged him to her, weeping softly, and, with a linen handkerchief, wiped at the tears that kept rolling down her face. "Tisha," she said between sobs, using the pet name she'd given him as a child, "it is still too soon, it is not yet time."

Though he knew that his mother had been dead for many years, that fact did not disturb him at all.

"The tsar has been waiting for an hour, Mama. We can't make him wait any longer."

And it was precisely this last detail that woke him: not so much that he was talking to his deceased mother as the fact that the tsar had come to their house and was waiting patiently for an invitation to enter. It was this that made him certain he was dreaming. Realizing it and waking up were practically a simultaneous occurrence. An instant before coming around, he could still make out the figure of the minister of culture shouldering a violin and drawing out the first notes of a popular cavatina . . .

■

HE OPENED HIS eyes. The wind was rattling the roll-up shutters. The rays of the setting sun filtered through the drawn curtains. Often his afternoon dreams were slow to dissolve, but this time the violin chords he heard, though mingled with the whistling of the wind through the window casings, were too audible to be the result of simple suggestion. Almost immediately, he recognized the exercises by Otakar Ševčík: his sister, Varvara, had practiced them each day with grueling dedication. There was a long moment of silence, then the first notes of a concerto with which he was also familiar rose up.

He leaped to his feet to listen. The sound came and went, sometimes clearly, sometimes covered by the wind's bluster. He moved along the walls until he found where it was coming from. There was no doubt about it: someone in the next room was playing the theme of Tchaikovsky's Violin Concerto. So there was another guest in the hotel, perhaps one who'd arrived that very morning, while he was out taking his walk. At the thought of someone with whom he might exchange a few words, Alekhine felt a certain excitement. By then, however, the chords had stopped, and in the lingering silence that followed, he was again seized by doubt: had it merely been a hallucination?

Recalling the dream he'd just had, he reached up to the bookshelf and took down a wooden case bound in Moroccan leather; it held the vase of Sèvres porcelain that he'd been given by the tsar in recognition of having won, at age sixteen, his first chess competition of some significance. He wanted to make sure it was still there. Each time, it was like opening the panels of an altarpiece. That object represented the highest honor that had ever been conferred on him; it was a talisman with which he would not part for any reason. He took it out to gaze at it. In the light of sunset that flooded the room, the blue surface took on intense hints of ruby red. Finally, he laid the vase carefully in its case and went back to the chessboard. His mind, however, kept returning to the violin he'd heard coming from the room next door.

He waited impatiently for the arrival of the boy who served him supper. Manuel was fifteen, rather self-confident for his age, and with Alekhine, for some reason, he usually made an effort to say a few words in German. During that month, the boy had told him all about his family and his ambitions. He was working to support himself while he studied, he explained, and when he grew up he was going to be a journalist. Often he approached the chessboard, observing the positions from time to time as though he understood the game, and every now and then he took the liberty of removing a book from the shelf and leafing through it while waiting to be sent on his way with a coin in his palm.

"Is there perhaps a new guest in the hotel?" Alekhine asked him now, feigning indifference.

"He's a violinist," the boy said, making the gesture of holding a violin. *"Er ist ein Geiger."*

III.

T HAT EVENING, ALEKHINE lingered in the lobby, expecting to meet the violinist. Who could say? Maybe, despite the gusty wind that discouraged going outside, he would come down to take a walk. After a while, however, Alekhine decided to return to his room. Climbing the stairs, he again felt a constriction in his chest. Angina pectoris—that was the precise name. By now he was becoming accustomed to tolerating the regular attacks. When he was back in his room, he tried tuning the radio to some foreign broadcast, but caught only snippets of popular music: aside from Dizzy Gillespie, Benny Goodman, and Artie Shaw, who were now all the rage on every frequency, the only thing he could manage to find was a mournful female voice singing Lusitanian *tristeza*.

The dream he'd had a few hours earlier had not completely faded, and the strains of that violin had transported him back in time. The house in Moscow, where he had spent his childhood, loomed up in his mind: he saw again the wooden parquet, its large squares scattered with Bokhara rugs; he saw the massive pendulum clock in the living room, the tiled stoves, the samovar with its copper reflections . . . He hadn't been back to Russia for decades, and perhaps his last words in that language had been spoken to his mother, his *mamushka*, before she went to die in a hospital bed. She was gravely ill, and when he'd approached her bedside she hardly recognized him. "It is still too soon. It is not yet time," she kept repeating. They were the same words he'd heard her say to him as a child, as she taught him his first concepts of chess: "It is still too soon to move that Pawn, it is not yet the right time to do it. You must wait. Be patient."

As a child, he'd been fascinated by the chessboard in an extraordinary way: it was as if a force released from underground had manifested itself on the surface, radiating through the geometries of the parquet at home, through the marble intarsia in the churches, the pavement of the streets and piazzas on which he walked. For him the flagstone paving had a magical aspect. The lines marking the porphyry slabs were never to be stepped on, for any reason. If just one were to crack under the weight of his foot—or so he imagined— the entire street and the piazza as well would somehow buckle, deformed by frightening alterations. The problem arose during walks along the streets of Moscow, when his sister, Varvara, held his hand and, not in the least suspecting his most hidden fears, tried to restrain him and make him walk in step. Besides having to avoid stepping on the lines, it was also necessary to place his foot precisely in the center of each square; some slabs might tilt under his weight and make him fall, or conceal other traps ready to swallow him up. Fortunately for him, the risky sections were almost always recognizable from a distance and therefore easily circumvented. Was the color of a given stone darker than the others? Was it streaked by veins? Did it have moss on its edges? Better not to step on it. And when Varvara, unaware of the danger, stubbornly refused to change course, leading him inexorably toward some fatal square—well, then, he was ultimately forced to leap ahead of her with a sudden tug on his sister's arm, catching her by surprise, and often putting her in danger of losing her balance.

"Stop jumping around like a billy goat," she scolded him. "Walk like a human being!"

The mania about not touching the seams, about staying in the center as much as possible, like a man balanced precariously on a floating plank, would soon be transferred to the chessboard. Observing the matches between Varvara and Aleksei, his older brother, he was already pained to see a Pawn, or any other piece, off-center. To him it seemed like inexcusable sloppiness, and in the end he couldn't resist the urge to adjust the pieces with a quick motion of his hand, even though he risked a slap: for him, the strict rule of "Look but don't touch" applied. This obsession had accompanied him throughout his life, up through his most recent match, to the point where, even in tournament competitions, he often couldn't help rearranging his own pieces during play, murmuring the ritual phrase "J'adoube," that is, "I'm adjusting it, I'm putting it in its place," a formula you had to follow so as not to be forced to move the piece that was thereby touched. At times, too, disturbed by the slightest asymmetry in the formation opposite him, he was even so bold as to make a sudden foray into the enemy ranks, with another "J'adoube," accompanied by a vaguely apologetic smile that disconcerted his opponent. He often wondered why no one had ever thought of obviating the problem by creating a slight circular hollow in the center of each square and, conversely, a convexity at the base of the pieces, a stratagem that would force them to remain in place. Finally, he bought a peg-type travel chess set in London, a chessboard meeting his precise requirements, which since then had become his faithful companion, immune to the jolts of a railway car as well as to the pitching of a steamship. It was the same chessboard that now sat there, on his table.

The person who had taught him all the rules of the game was his mother, holding him on her lap so he would have the same perspective. As soon as he was able to play, his older siblings, Varvara and Aleksei, became his first opponents—especially Varvara, who was the more willing, whereas Aleksei still treated him with disdain and, whenever he could, avoided him. At that time, the game of chess had seemed to him like a complex mechanical system operated by levers and buttons. To move even a single Pawn in the farthest corner of the chessboard meant setting in motion gears and balance wheels that kept changing the existing order; two distinct mechanisms ended up merging into one, and wrong moves screeched like seized-up cogs. Even then he adored the paradoxical movement of the Knights, supporting each other, like two trapeze artists circling in the air. He had often wondered, in the fictional battle, what the fate of the captured pieces was, but the answer was always the same: the game of chess was a war that left no prisoners behind.

He was seven years old then, and chess was still a board game like many others, though immensely more complex. For a few years, he would continue to play during school vacations or on long Sunday afternoons when bad weather made it inadvisable to leave the house. Nevertheless, though his love for chess was great, he was held back by a fear that the game, no matter how incomparably beautiful, was destined to remain a simple recreational activity, set within the domestic walls, and therefore did not warrant his complete devotion.

His real inspiration arrived a few years later, when, together with Varvara and Aleksei, he had witnessed an unprecedented performance. In a theater in St. Petersburg, he was able to admire Harry Nelson

Pillsbury, the American champion, take part in a simultaneous blindfold match against twenty-four strong players. For the entire duration of the show, as he followed the game of the young Yankee—who, sitting in an armchair with his back to the contenders, smoked one cigar after another and, without seeing the chessboards, responded promptly to every move—little Aleksandr had felt such excitement that, once he was back home, his temperature had risen to 104 degrees. He was kept in bed for two days. The family doctor was called in, though the physician was quick to reassure them all about the boy's condition: the fever was likely due to indigestion, or to a chill. Not even a doctor could imagine that the cause had simply been the child's feverish emotion at recognizing the enormity of what until then he had considered only a pastime. The image of the young American, who, with a sure, steady voice, routed one after another of his stunned opponents, would never leave him. Nothing like the analyses made at the table with his brother, Aleksei, the lackluster games with his sister, Varvara—they were a joke! Pillsbury's performance was the true game of chess! In fact, chess wasn't a game, it was an art. And in those two days spent in bed, Aleksandr Alekhin made up his mind that he would devote himself entirely to that art.

IV.

AND SO, AS always after his afternoon nap, he was once again sitting in front of the chessboard. After the meeting with the man from Lisbon, he had taken to analyzing the games of the two probable candidates to challenge him for the world championship: one was the Estonian Paul Keres, and the other the Russian Mikhail Botvinnik, both prominent exponents of the new generation of Soviet chess, both prepared, both formidable. Of the two, however, Botvinnik was the one with the greatest likelihood of officially representing the Soviet Union. As far back as '39, in fact, he had sent Alekhine a written challenge, but following the outbreak of the world war their match was canceled. Alekhine had played three games against him: one, in Nottingham in '36, ended in a draw; a couple of years later, at a tournament organized by a major Dutch radio station, he had tied another match playing White and then lost one with Black. It was the moves in the latter game that he was now analyzing, with the intention of improving his defense. He spent most of the night intent on disassembling and reconstructing that crucial defeat. He would often sit in front of the chessboard until very late, only drifting off to sleep at the first light of dawn. As he slept, however, he continued moving the pieces on a faintly recalled chessboard. That morning, as he was about to wake up, the solution seemed quite close: an absolutely new idea, which unfortunately quickly vanished. It was as if he had grasped the mythical phoenix by the tail a moment before it went up in flames.

He found himself still sitting in the armchair—another night without going to bed. He had no idea how long he'd slept. In the complex arrangement of the pieces left on the chessboard, he immediately recognized the result of the analysis he had been conducting until a few hours earlier. Sleep, however, aside from that somewhat dreamlike illumination that had so swiftly evaporated, had not brought insight: his position was still damnably complicated, and he had not yet found a variant favorable to him.

■

AFTER BREAKFAST, HE walked along the beach, but instead of going toward the lighthouse, he chose the opposite direction, toward Tubarão: a tavern down a back alley, near a cove where a flotilla of fishing boats was moored. The day was mild and calm. The strong wind of the day before had dwindled to a gentle breeze.

It was Sunday morning, and after the ten o'clock Mass, the place, already filled with smoke, was jammed with people. Most of them came from the fishermen's village. They also played chess there. The stakes were generally a couple of cigarettes, but could be raised several times during the game if such was proposed by one of the players: a person who thought he was winning tended to accept, and often offered a counterproposal in turn. The trick was to gull your opponent into believing he had a winning position, or at least a solid one. In short, to bluff, as in poker. For Alekhine winning would be child's play, but he didn't want to trick anyone. He had been to the tavern several times, merely as a spectator until, one day, an old fisherman with a frizzy iron-gray beard invited him to play. The challenger had immediately placed a couple of *cigarros nacionais* beside the chessboard, and Alekhine had done the same. As always, Alekhine felt obliged to politely inform the opponent that he was unbeatable, and therefore in a position to offer him an advantage; at this, the fisherman had turned to the rest of the room and, reporting the proposal aloud, provoked general hilarity. The challenger was surely considered a strong player, since a small knot of curious onlookers were already crowded around the table, rooting for their champion.

Indulging the fisherman, parrying his sporadic attacks here and there, Alekhine avoided taking advantage of the various occasions when he could have concluded the game with a checkmate, settling for a Pawn ending: wanting thereby to make the man think he had won by a narrow margin. The victory, seemingly narrow, put him in a bad mood, however. He couldn't explain to himself why he had done it. So as not to humiliate the man in front of his buddies? To amuse himself, like a cat with a mouse? On balance, he thought, he had demeaned the game by playing that way.

"*Vingança?*" the man had proposed with an uncertain smile.

"*A próxima vez*," he had replied, getting up from the table.

He left the tavern with an inexplicable sense of prostration. Somehow he felt he had committed a grave sin, as if he'd defiled a sacred icon. Was it admissible—he wondered—to stoop to that level? Was it right to recite a poem by Pushkin to an illiterate, or expound a philosophical principle to an imbecile? One should not cast pearls before swine, lest they trample them under their feet, and turn against you, reads the Gospel. In his moments of unreasonable intolerance, he often came to the conclusion that access to all the arts should have remained the privilege of the few who were able to appreciate them. And the same for chess. Inclined to shun the common herd and the places where it congregated, he took comfort in his dreams of domination and supremacy, the better to conquer the loathing that the masses roused in him—the only remedy that made him feel still alive among the dead.

■

THAT SUNDAY, HOWEVER, he decided to return to the Tubarão with very different intentions. He wanted to show them all how chess should be played. He had brought two packs of Caporals in anticipation of a challenge—a more than sufficient supply.

As soon as he took the three steps down into the tavern, which was packed as usual, the din abruptly died down and everyone fell silent, looking up at him. The innkeeper ceremoniously invited him to the bar and, after wiping his hands on his soiled apron, filled a glass of red wine to the brim and offered it to him with a comical, theatrical bow. Finally, the innkeeper turned to those in the room: "*Vamos fazer um brinde ao campeão mundial de xadrez!*" he said loudly, urging the onlookers to toast.

Greeted with that unexpected welcome, Alekhine felt disoriented—it had every appearance of being a solemn farce. Nevertheless, he decided to respond to the toast. It was really odd, he thought. If they were pulling his leg, they had to be acting under someone's direction: it seemed unlikely that they could have orchestrated it themselves, that all of them, from the innkeeper down to the last customer, were staging this performance with the sole intent of mocking him. Moreover, he saw no trace of ridicule in the eyes of those present, and even the old fisherman who had challenged him on his previous visit was staring at him with an expression of respect and admiration. Meanwhile, after wiping a rag over the bar counter, which was smudged with circles and crescents, the innkeeper carefully unfolded a page from the *Diário de Lisboa*. There Alekhine immediately recognized a photo of himself; though it had been taken a few years earlier, it was still a good likeness. The article took up half a page, announcing the upcoming match for the world title. As he'd expected, the challenger was Mikhail Botvinnik. Abruptly, he no longer heard or saw anything around him: there was only the sheet of newspaper, which his eyes scanned eagerly. The stakes, the article's author reported, were ten thousand dollars, and as holder of the title he was entitled to choose the location of the match. Rather than Nottingham, he would prefer London, where he still had acquaintances. As for the date, as soon as possible! By now he was tired of this involuntary holiday. He could only hope that the contentious speech given by Winston Churchill a few weeks earlier—about the "iron curtain" dividing the continent—would not rekindle hostilities between Europe and the Soviet Union, thereby thwarting the long-awaited challenge for the second time.

■

HE WASN'T PERMITTED to leave the tavern until he had taken part in countless toasts. After all those glasses of *vinhozinho*, anyone else would have staggered out of the place; for him it would have taken quite a bit more. He felt only slightly euphoric at the news. Finally, he would make his return to the world stage, and although the challenger was the most formidable of opponents, his ego inspired in him the certainty of being the best player of all time. Of course, no chess player, no matter how well prepared, would be capable of stepping onto the world stage without trusting his inner conviction of being the best, and Botvinnik undoubtedly thought the very same thing. The difference was that the Russian champion seemed like a lion prodded by a trident and forcibly driven into the arena. Standing behind him was the Soviet system, to which he was answerable. The responsibility was enormous for a young man of thirty-four. Botvinnik was now under the aegis and the yoke of "Little Father" Stalin, who did not readily tolerate being disappointed by his children. After the deaths of Capablanca, Lasker, Nimzowitsch, and other talented chess players, there weren't many other prominent names remaining in the Western world who could oppose the Soviet Union, which conversely boasted of turning out the best players on the planet. Only he remained, Aleksandr Aleksandrovich Alekhin, the last bastion: if Botvinnik were able to beat him, the younger man would be proving to the world, once and for all, the supremacy of the Soviet school. Making the match even more exciting was that it would be two Russians competing, not only from different generations, but also with contrasting views and ideals: a dissident versus a strong supporter of the system. Botvinnik had to win at all costs, or risk losing the privileges he'd acquired—and that, Alekhine thought, might very well be his Achilles' heel.

He returned to the hotel with a sense of buoyancy that he hadn't felt for a long time. Even the staircase seemed less strenuous than usual; as he climbed the steps, he noticed only a slight fluttering of his heart, like an affectionate reproach. He imagined that some of the staff would have read the newspaper and spread the news. What in fact gave him the greatest satisfaction, besides winning, was the approbation of his admirers; his long period of inactivity had depressed him no less than the solitude. Among the hotel's employees, however, he didn't notice any difference in behavior.

Nonetheless, there was a new development: for the first time since he'd been staying at the hotel, he saw, on a couch in the lobby, a man whom he had never seen before. It must be the mysterious violinist who occupied the room next to his. He was in his forties, small in stature, with a mass of blondish hair that must once have been thick and was now thinning. He was wearing gray corduroy pants, a flannel shirt with dolman sleeves, and a colorful scarf. Sitting comfortably on the couch, surrounded by the pages of a musical score that he had spread out around him, he was making notes on one sheet with a pencil stub. He was so focused that he wasn't immediately aware of Alekhine's presence. When he finally looked up and saw the master, he sprang quickly to his feet—scattering his papers—and, as if he'd been expecting him, came forward with a broad smile. Alekhine wasn't surprised: two castaways who meet on an island are quick to become friends.

"Allow me to introduce myself," the man began, extending a slim hand. "I am David Neumann, and I sincerely hope that I did not disturb you yesterday afternoon. My fault: I didn't think to inform the management that I might trouble someone with my violin . . ."

Alekhine thought he could make out the guttural inflections typical of the Flemish language in the man's voice.

"No bother, believe me. Your music took me back to my childhood, when I would listen to my sister, Varvara, practicing the violin."

Neumann became serious: "If there are certain times when you would prefer strict quiet, don't hesitate to tell me. And if you prefer, I can ask the management to assign me a room on another floor."

"As far as I'm concerned, you can even practice in the middle of the night. Especially if it means listening to the music of the great Tchaikovsky."

"I see with satisfaction that you are obviously an authority on music as well as chess . . . because you are the celebrated Alekhine, are you not?" And, noting Alekhine's surprised reaction, he quickly added: "I read the news in the *Diário de Lisboa.*"

At those words, Alekhine was flooded with a wave of warm satisfaction. "So you play chess? In addition to playing the violin, I mean."

Neumann laughed, blushing: "No, no, not at all. I only played chess as a child. The real enthusiast was my father, a great admirer of yours. I still remember the boundless interest with which he followed all the games of the 1927 match you played against that Cuban . . . what was his name?"

"Capablanca," Alekhine muttered. He would have preferred not to have to pronounce that name; it made him irritable just to hear it.

"My father had a friend in Buenos Aires who telegraphed him the moves of each game. It was a memorable encounter, wasn't it?"

"Truly memorable."

What he actually wanted to say was "A match to forget." And he would have forgotten it, if only there weren't always someone to remind him of it.

■

IT HAD BEEN almost twenty years since that titanic battle had taken place, lasting more than two months, through thirty-four grueling games. A skirmish from which Alekhine had finally emerged victorious—winning the world championship crown—but which had also depleted him, draining him of every ounce of energy. For Capablanca "the invincible," the defeat had been a crushing blow. At the resumption of the last, decisive game, which had been left unfinished the day before at the fortieth move, the Cuban champion hadn't even had the courage to show his face in the tournament room, and had merely sent a message in which he announced his definitive withdrawal.

Although Capablanca was rightfully entitled to a return match, Alekhine—citing the choice of venue or insufficient prize money—found every excuse to postpone the encounter. He had even avoided participating in tournaments in which the Cuban was present. Rather than square off with him again, he'd have played with the devil himself. And though Capablanca continued to protest, demanding what was rightfully his, Alekhine had hastily arranged a few matches with less aggressive opponents, even readily accepting the resounding defeat he suffered at the hands of the Dutchman Max Euwe. And so, at least for the time required to organize a return match, he had been safe from his challenger's demands—demands that Capablanca had insistently renewed after Alekhine had regained the title in 1937, and which persisted until the Cuban's death four years ago, in 1942, from a stroke that he suffered while he was at the Manhattan Chess Club observing a friendly game. The news of Capablanca's death had removed a weight from Alekhine's chest; nevertheless, he could not help mourning the passing of his chosen opponent, who at one time had been a friend, but who in the end had become the man he most hated and feared.

■

"ARE YOU FEELING all right, Dr. Alekhine?"

He realized that he must have a very strange expression on his face if the violinist thought to ask him that question.

"Yes, of course. Why?" he replied curtly.

"I hope, Dr. Alekhine, that I have not awakened painful memories for you."

"No, not at all. The match in Buenos Aires was a wonderful experience," he said, forcing himself to assume a relaxed, even cheerful air.

A waiter arrived, letting him off the hook, and informed them that, in anticipation of new arrivals, the dining room would return to partial operation starting the following day. There was always, however, the option of calling room service. Neumann glanced questioningly at Alekhine, who confirmed, in a mildly condescending tone, "Tomorrow evening I will gladly go down for dinner."

Neumann simply nodded yes.

V.

ALEKHINE WENT UP to his room, where he was served lunch. He hardly touched any of the food under the heavy silver domes: his stomach was churning, partly because of the wine he'd drunk at the tavern, but mainly because of what lay ahead. He wondered if he would have enough time to prepare properly. All of a sudden, he felt like a student on the eve of exams, fearful that he's forgotten everything. For years, he'd been following the playing style of the young Soviet prodigy. Over time, he had assembled data on all of Botvinnik's most important games, and by now he had memorized them, along with every possible variant. He was thoroughly familiar with the man's strategy; unless his seconds had prepared some surprise opening for

him, he was certain that Botvinnik would start the game by moving his Queen's Pawn. Alekhine had no doubts as to what defense to adopt. He had no choice but to find a convincing line of attack to be put forward by White, and in this he relied on his unerring instinct; he was always able to seize upon any favorable opportunity in the thick of the game.

He lingered at length in front of the mirror. To start with, he had to look like his old self again. In recent weeks, he, who had always been so attentive to his elegance, had neglected his attire: his suits were crumpled, his ties hopelessly wrinkled, and of all the shirts he owned there wasn't one that he could still wear without feeling a bit embarrassed. He opened the big wardrobe and emptied it completely, tossing its contents on the bed. He selected two daywear suits and one for evening. Then he called the laundress, and gave her precise instructions: at least one dark suit and a shirt had to be ready as soon as possible. When she had gone, he locked the door, put on his smoking jacket, and sank into the roomy armchair. From there, from that very spot, a gigantic task was beginning for him, perhaps the last great challenge of his life. He was too much of an optimist to deny that he had a chance to win, too experienced not to realize that his chances were narrow. Though the god of chess was generally propitious, at times it could be quite formidable.

HE SPENT SEVERAL hours at the chessboard, repeatedly starting over and repeatedly reaching the same point. The more he studied this position, the more convinced he was that to solve the problem he had to widen the scope of his research, not just going back a decade, as he had done, but also, as far as was possible, projecting into the future, to anticipate forthcoming developments. That would mean advancing into a no-man's-land, where anything could happen. Never before had he felt so disoriented. There was something about the young Soviet whiz kid's game that Alekhine could not grasp, or even define, except as a perfect blend of the old Russian school, inspired by the game of attack, and the more modern ideas that had spread in recent years. Mikhail Botvinnik was an electrical engineer, and was able to bring together in his game both a romantic fervor, belonging to a glorious past, and a technological rigor that represented the future of chess.

·

NOT A SOUND from Neumann that afternoon. Evidently, he was reluctant to disturb the silence; perhaps he had applied a damper to the instrument and was stroking the strings so lightly that only he could hear the results.

Toward evening, Alekhine sank into sleep. He dreamed of walking along a path in a park headed for a young man who was sitting on a bench. When he came within a few steps, he recognized the young man as Raúl Capablanca. The light in that dream was as bright as a floodlight, so that every detail of Capablanca's figure stood out with extreme vividness: Alekhine imagined that he could make out the fabric of his jacket, the irregularity of a mother-of-pearl button, chipped on the edge, or the frayed threads of his worn shirt cuff. Raúl was smiling seraphically, as always; with those big, childlike eyes of his, he looked like the image of a saint.

·

THE ARRIVAL OF the waiter with the food cart woke him. From the way the young man looked at him, he could tell that his photo in the *Diário de Lisboa* had by now made the rounds of the hotel. The boy said very little, and, unlike on his other visits, when he would make a joke or two, he was extremely respectful. He discreetly removed the dishes, still untouched, from lunch, and served Alekhine his dinner, but this time, in addition to the usual bottle of Alentejo, a bottle of champagne had been provided, in a bucket with ice, courtesy of the management.

Alekhine ate listlessly, but sipped the champagne with pleasure: a luxury he had not allowed himself for some time. He hadn't managed to finish the bottle before there was another knock on the door. It was the woman with the ironing, returning two suits that looked as good as new, two shirts, washed and starched, and several brand-new ties. To reward her solicitude, he gave up the last escudos he had in his pocket.

VI.

THE NIGHT PASSED quietly. After taking a hot bath and swallowing two tablets of Veronal, Alekhine had actually managed to fall asleep in his bed. His excitement had abruptly subsided, enabling him to sink into a dreamless sleep. He woke up completely refreshed, and in a good mood as well, a rarity for him. He shaved carefully, put on a clean shirt and his best suit.

Stepping into the hall to pick up his shoes, which he found polished to a sheen each morning, he discovered a large yellow envelope, rather hefty, that someone had left at his door. Inside were several newspaper clippings in various languages. This did not surprise him: he had in fact complained to the management about the total lack of foreign papers there. Someone had obviously remedied the deficiency in his own way. He leafed through the contents of the envelope. The majority of the articles had to do with the Nuremberg trials. This was not surprising, either, given the current burning interest in the subject. He placed the envelope on the shelf where he kept his books, intending to read the articles later on.

■

THAT MORNING, ON his walk to the lighthouse, he saw Neumann watching something intently at the water's edge. The musician was wearing a lizard-green overcoat, a vicuña scarf wrapped around his neck, and a *purillo* on his head. Not until Alekhine was a few steps away from him did Neumann become aware of his presence. The object that had completely absorbed his attention was the shell of a tortoise that the surf had driven ashore.

"Good morning, Dr. Alekhine," he exclaimed, taken by surprise.

"Good morning to you, maestro. I missed the sound of your violin yesterday afternoon."

"I'm sorry, but sometimes it's necessary to work out a piece on the printed score rather than on the strings."

Alekhine nodded.

"I imagine you're here for a concert."

"Next Sunday, I play with the Lisbon Philharmonic Orchestra— the Tchaikovsky concerto."

"If I can, I will come to applaud you."

Meanwhile, the violinist had fallen in step with him. It was only natural for two people heading in the same direction, but Neumann was hesitant.

"I hope you don't mind if I walk a little way with you."

"Not at all."

Yet Neumann did not yet seem entirely reassured.

"You know, sometimes one would rather be alone, to reflect, especially in anticipation of a big event like the one that awaits you . . ."

"Not in the least. It's been a month since I've exchanged a word with . . . another living being."

At that point, Neumann found the courage to strike a more personal note: "I assume you began playing as a child."

"Yes, it was my mother who first taught me the basics. But my sister, Varvara, and my brother, Aleksei, also played chess well. Aleksei was quite gifted, and for some time I was forced to endure one defeat after another. Our house was frequently visited by great Russian chess players, such as Bogolyubov and Znosko-Borovsky, who often gave me private lessons as well."

To Neumann those names meant nothing.

"Tell me, if I'm not being too inquisitive, is there such a thing as a perfect move in chess?"

"What do you mean?"

Neumann blushed, flustered: "A perfect game, rather."

Alekhine thought that, as much as he liked the violinist's company, he had no desire to start explaining his vision of the game to him. He could, perhaps, bring the conversation around to music, and get even with the violinist by asking him what correlation there was between the sound of the violin and the music of the spheres, or between the vibrations of a note above high C and the collapse of the walls of Jericho. He refrained from being cruel, however.

"It's difficult to say. There is always some detail whose presence is capable of altering the entire scheme of things."

Neumann nodded thoughtfully. Actually, Alekhine knew perfectly well that those words could apply to everything, even to life in general. For a while they continued walking in silence. When they were near the lighthouse, they stopped a few minutes to observe the flight of hundreds of petrels that were filling the air with their deafening screeches.

On the way back, Neumann spoke again.

"My father used to say that chess is a mixture of technique and art."

"Indeed, that's so," Alekhine confirmed. "All the arts share a common effort to dominate matter, to bring order to chaos. Technique comes to our aid to perform that task, but beyond that there is an additional factor that enables a work to rise to the level of art."

"Just as with music."

"Precisely. Except that, unlike the other arts, which seek to shape inert material, chess must come to grips with a magmatic mass that is constantly evolving. I am referring to the opponent's game, which very often is far from being in tune with our own. Winning the match in that case brings no satisfaction. But when the two are in perfect accord, one is even willing to relinquish a victory in order not to spoil the perfect aesthetics of the game. Still, even under the most favorable conditions, the tyranny of time often leads us to make some slipup, causing the whole structure to suddenly collapse."

"Listening to what you say, I realize that I never thought about chess that way."

Now it seemed Neumann did not want to get too entangled in a subject that was beyond him. He merely circled around it.

"So you are convinced that to excel in chess one must have a predisposition, a genuine innate talent?"

"Of course. A person can study the openings and endgames all he wants. By applying himself, he might become a good player and even draw a certain satisfaction from chess. But the world of the great soloists is never very crowded. Don't you agree?"

■

WHEN THEY WERE near the hotel, Neumann decided to continue on toward the harbor. They left each other with an awkward handshake.

Alekhine found himself thinking that the man was quite likable. Despite his surname, which clearly disclosed his race.

Back at the hotel, Alekhine stopped by the reception desk as usual. This time, the clerk was beaming. He produced a letter. Alekhine saw at once that the sender was Francisco Lupi, whom he had asked for help.

"Thank the manager for the articles," he said with detached politeness.

"Articles? What articles?"

"Someone left an envelope at my door, containing various newspaper articles."

"I will pass on your thanks to the management," the clerk said with a puzzled air.

Alekhine withdrew to a corner of the lobby. In the envelope, along with some banknotes, was a note from Lupi.

> *Dear Alexandre,*
>
> *Please forgive my delay in replying to your letter, but I just got back a few days ago. I read the wonderful news. Finally, you are back in the spotlight!*
>
> *With regard to your request to write some articles, for the moment it is not possible, but I think you must now have other things on your mind. In any case, I am enclosing some money "for cigarettes," and will see to it that you get more shortly. Count on me for anything you need. Meanwhile, be aware that you will soon receive a visit from a reporter. Her name is Teresa Ocampo, and she works for the* Diário de Lisboa. *She wants to do a long interview about your life and your career.*
>
> *Know that I am ready, whenever you'd like, to come and see you. It would be my pleasure to be your second and help you devise a good variant for White.*
>
> *Meanwhile, I send my best regards,*

Francisco
P.S. You will be appropriately compensated for the interview.

Alekhine counted the money and headed purposefully toward the bar. This called for a drink to celebrate. At the last moment, though, he had second thoughts, and after phoning the newspaper office to agree on the date and time of the interview, he decided to go up to his room. As he was leaving the elevator, the porter passed by, pushing a cart full of bags and suitcases.

So there were new guests, he thought. But he wasn't sure that he was especially pleased about it.

VII.

H E MET THEM that same night. It was the first evening when he would not be dining in his room, and he'd chosen the dark double-breasted jacket for the occasion. Several tables had been laid in the dining room. The new arrivals, a middle-aged couple, were already seated, sipping white wine. After greeting them with a slight bow, Alekhine sat at the next table. He was able to observe them more closely from there. They were both in their sixties. The man was rather small and plump, with flabby, red-veined cheeks and extensive baldness offset by thick graying side-whiskers. Alekhine thought that, with a Scottish-plaid waistcoat and an apron tied around his waist, he would have made a striking figure behind the bar of a pub in London's West End.

His companion was draped in an elegant, amaranth-colored evening dress, which bared her shoulders and back, the shoulder blades sharp like the rapacious profile of her face. If she had ever been young, she had certainly never been beautiful. Her only glory was thick, raven-colored hair with blue glints.

Neumann entered shortly after, having donned a tuxedo to mark the occasion. After offering a timid greeting, he hesitated as to what seat to take, until Alekhine came to his rescue, pointing to the chair in front of him: that way, wishing to avoid any contact with the new-comers, he would not be forced to stare into space.

The new man, however, seemed eager to strike up a conversation, and as soon as he caught Alekhine's eye, raised his glass welcomingly. "Dr. Alekhine, allow me to introduce myself: I am Jorge Correira, and this is my wife. I feel truly honored. I never thought I would one day find myself dining in the company of the world chess champion."

There was a vague trace of irony in the man's querulous voice that made it irritating.

"And with a great violinist as well," Alekhine responded, indicating Neumann, who began to demur.

"Ah, music and chess!" the other exclaimed. "What extraordinary similarities and differences in those two arts. Although my wife was a talented soprano, I myself understand little about music. I enjoy listening to it, but my knowledge is limited to the seven notes—don't ask me anything more. As a young man, however, I was a great enthusiast of chess, and even now I get to play a few games, albeit as an amateur."

As always when he found himself dealing with a fan, Alekhine tried not to appear standoffish.

"I hope you still take pleasure in it."

"Oh yes, I still consider myself a decent player, although a bit rusty," the man quickly replied, with a certain smugness. "In fact, I would be genuinely honored to be able to cross swords with you, if it's not asking too much."

"I shall be happy to oblige," Alekhine replied with the formal tone he used on such occasions.

The waiter arrived with the entrées that the Correiras had already ordered: a kind of beef stew, and veal chops with mushrooms. Soon afterward, the sommelier came in cradling a bottle of red wine in both hands—as if it were a baby—which Senhor Correira tasted and approved with the air of a connoisseur. After which he motioned to the waiter to serve the wine to the neighboring table.

"Dr. Alekhine, tell me what you think of this Aragonês; it's a 1937."

Alekhine took a sip.

"What do you think?"

"I think it's superb."

"Did you know that Portuguese winemakers resort to a curious method to give the Aragonês the unique flavor that sets it apart?"

"And what would that be?"

"Have you noticed that in Portugal there are more stray dogs than inhabitants?"

"Indeed, I see quite a few ambling along the beach."

"When they form a pack, they become dangerous, for both people and livestock. The locals do not hesitate to shoot them, or club them to death, and then they like to leave the bodies to rot in the ditches bordering the vineyards. A good way to deal with the carcasses, don't you think?"

Alekhine smiled. He couldn't tell if the man was serious, but for some reason, that word, "carcasses," thrown out so casually, had felt deliberate.

"Is that so? In any case, it seems to me to be an excellent vintage," he remarked.

"It was also an excellent year for you . . ." Correira observed with a knowing air. "That was the year you regained the title, if I'm not mistaken."

"Yes, that's right, it was in '37," Alekhine confirmed. Perhaps

Senhor Correira was hoping to continue this line of conversation, but Alekhine's attention was distracted by the waiter who had approached to take his order, and that was the end of the matter. For the remainder of the dinner, the conversation focused on wines and foods, but sooner or later, no doubt, Correira would return to the topic of chess. And, in fact, when they had reached dessert, he very casually turned to Alekhine, as if they had never stopped talking about it, and said: "What do you think of this Botvinnik, who's the leading light of the new Soviet school? I seem to remember that you lost a match with him."

Alekhine tried to suppress the irritation he always felt when having to admit defeat, particularly when hearing anyone talk about the "new Soviet school."

"Surely a promising young man," he replied briefly. "However, I don't believe it's correct to speak of a 'new Soviet school' . . . or, at any rate, I tend to associate such terminology with the typical language of Bolshevik propaganda."

"I don't follow you."

"It's quite simple. After the October Revolution, the Bolsheviks arrogated to themselves the right to divulge *their own* truth. Just as in life, in finance, and in the world of art and ideas, so, too, in chess. Russia has given the world great chess players—Alapin, Chigorin, Romanovsky, Znosko-Borovsky . . . These were masters who had a great influence; they all had a very lofty conception of chess. But you will certainly never hear exponents of the elusive 'new Soviet school' talk about beauty or genius. Chess for them is a kind of collective war machine, and they themselves are nothing more than a close-knit phalanx of underlings. The individual no longer exists, even in chess, only the masses. Every victory achieved by one of their champions is merely the result of the scrupulous training of hundreds of bureaucrats of the game."

"I discern a certain bitterness in you when you speak of your compatriots," Correira persisted, with a malicious gleam in his eye. "Yet, if I am not mistaken, you yourself were a member of the Communist Party."

"Yes, I was for a period of time," Alekhine admitted, lowering his voice slightly. "You could only play chess at my level with a party card in your pocket. Then, too, in that situation, I had every opportunity to observe what was going on."

"Indeed, the observer of the game who doesn't miss a thing!" Correira exclaimed cheerfully. "It's merely a question of understanding what the game is," he added, sinking his spoon into his creamy dessert. His wife, meanwhile, had hardly touched her food, or uttered a single word. "Tell me, Dr. Alekhine, with regard to strategies . . . what did you do during the war?"

"Perhaps you mean 'during the wars.' Because I was caught up in two wars, and though I was still young and full of vigor when the first one ended, the second one took everything out of me," he replied. As he said those words, his voice became emotional. "The game of chess is the only thing I still have left, the only thing that is able to drive away my most painful memories."

But Correira seemed determined to tighten the screws.

"You, however, emerged from it all unscathed."

"What do you mean?" Alekhine asked, darkening.

"I am referring to those with whom you associated. You were able to get by all right in any situation," Correira said mildly.

"In '39, when news arrived that the Nazis had invaded Poland, I was in Buenos Aires. At the time, I was leading the French lineup, and I refused to play against the German team. That should make clear what my position was toward them."

"And yet, a few years later, you played in the lead group, under the shadow of the swastika—"

Alekhine didn't let him finish.

"Keep in mind that to save one's life one is sometimes forced to make compromises, to dress up in the enemy's clothing. I did everything possible to go on playing chess. I was never interested in politics. When chess was discouraged altogether in Russia, because it was considered bourgeois, I took refuge in France and enlisted in the French army. With the Nazi occupation, I had to allow myself to be bought, in the hopes of obtaining a visa for my wife to leave the country."

"In any case, one should never come to terms with the enemy, isn't that so?" Correira observed insinuatingly.

"Frankly, I have no regrets. We were at war. Yes, it's true, to keep my ration card I had to play for the Nazi team. But for me chess has no political color. I don't know what else you're alluding to. What could I have done? Escape? Go into hiding? Do you think that if I'd had the chance to get out of the occupied territories I would have stayed to play for their flag?"

Correira, as if to lighten the mood, laughed. But it was too merry a laugh, too strident to be natural.

"No, no, whatever are you thinking? I don't blame you at all. Without a stamp on one's passport one can't get very far. I know this from experience," he said, turning to his spouse with a look full of tenderness. "My wife is Jewish. During the war, we lived in Paris. After the occupation, we decided to flee to the Free Zone and procure a visa to the United States. On the way, we miraculously escaped a roundup—but, because of the shock she suffered, my wife lost her voice. From that time on, not only has she been unable to sing, but to this day she can barely speak more than a few words."

The woman raised her eyes and stared into Alekhine's, then abruptly ran her index finger across her throat. The gesture made him shiver, calling to mind a bogeyman from his childhood: a beggar, afflicted with macromelia, who often roamed around their neighborhood, dragging along a big sack into which he crammed anything useful he could find. He liked to frighten children by threatening to put them in his bag, and when he encountered someone in the street he would run his index finger across his throat: a gesture fraught with dark forebodings. People claimed he was just a harmless madman, but later, after the masses had come to power, Alekhine would see him again, tidy and clean-shaven, in the garb of an official in one of the many ministerial offices.

"I have had other misfortunes . . ." Alekhine said, trailing off.

A heavy silence fell, which Senhor Correira decided to dispel by proposing a toast. He signaled to the sommelier—a caryatid who had remained standing in a corner this entire time—and ordered him to open the bottle of champagne already placed on ice for the occasion.

"A toast to the everlasting world champion!"

Alekhine reluctantly complied. The odd man's invitation sounded false to him. Almost ominous.

VIII.

T HROUGHOUT THE DINNER, Neumann had not said a single word, and
now, as they walked together through the deserted lobby, he appeared to be in a somber mood. It was clear that Correira's words had
troubled him.

"A real charmer, that man," he remarked finally, shaking his head.
"He seemed to have something against you."

"He's not the only one."

"I'm going to take a little walk before going up to my room," Neumann said.

Alekhine understood that he preferred to be alone. "Good
night, then. And, by the way," he added, "don't think twice about

practicing . . . Remember what I told you: I adore the sound of the violin—at any time of day." But as soon as he said it, he cursed himself for this gauche attempt to ingratiate himself.

Neumann smiled sadly and walked toward the exit. Alekhine's gaze followed the small figure, smartly dressed in his tuxedo, perhaps the same one he wore when performing in a concert. Suddenly, Alekhine was seized with a great urge to have a strong drink, but the bar was closed at that hour: a faint bluish light illuminated the rows of bottles lined up on the shelf behind the counter, like so many votive candles.

As he retrieved his room key, the clerk handed Alekhine a note informing him of the time of his meeting with the journalist. Miss Ocampo had phoned confirming her arrival the following morning at ten.

Alekhine went up to his room. It gnawed at him that Neumann had witnessed that painful conversation at dinner. After the evening spent with Senhor Correira and his unspeakable wife, he felt vaguely uneasy. The dinner had left him with an ominous feeling. He kept wondering what on earth that strange individual could possibly want from him.

He shook off these thoughts and returned to his chessboard, almost as though to reassure himself that in the meantime no one had altered the position of the pieces, which had been left at the crucial point of the game he had played against Botvinnik a decade earlier. He remained there, as motionless and inscrutable as a sphinx. Each piece, placed on its own square, was like an image in a painting that at first glance is reassuring in its striking veracity, but that, once you observe it more closely, reveals another image, darker than the first, though analogous, as a reflection might be, or a shadow.

Though it was an essential task, armchair analysis of the matches he'd played in the past often bored him. Without the presence of the human element, the pieces on the chessboard lost their vitality. It was quite a different matter to play with an opponent in front of you: to enter his mind, predict his strategies by interpreting the slightest variations of his posture, the position of his hands, the subtle though significant contractions of his lips. During the period when he worked for the Moscow police, they had taught Alekhine how to interpret small signs such as these during interrogations, to see if their subjects were lying.

■

FROM THE ROOM next door came the sound of violin chords. Hearing them, Alekhine felt a sense of relief, as if, through his music, Neumann were expressing solidarity with him. He imagined that the notes represented a kind of bond between the two of them, which sanctioned the start of an empathy perhaps even destined to lead to a tentative friendship. But had he, Alekhine, ever had a friend among the Jews? No more than those he could count among the Gentiles. Added to this question was another, more ruthless one: had he ever had any true friends? Few, very few, he had to admit. And yet he was aware of a new feeling toward the small Jewish violinist. It was the first sign of emotional neediness, a need to fill a void, a sense of detachment, a wish to reminisce with Neumann about bygone times, perhaps experienced together in a now vanished Arcadia. That's how he had always imagined the world of art: a lofty, inaccessible place, below which the wretched masses rushed about unceasingly. The latter, joining forces in the effort, had finally managed to reach the top and dethrone the rightful inhabitants, leaving in the wake of their disastrous passage the toppled statues of deities, heads severed, their shattered noses and eyes filled with crumbling soil. The artists in exile, now scattered throughout the world, recognized one another when they met, and no religion or ideology could keep them apart.

HE TRIED TO focus on the game. Every so often, however, Correira's image loomed up before him. Why was that man so interested in his past? What gave Correira the right to question him so arrogantly, with the insistence of an inquisitor? That mellifluous way of investigating the facts of his life made Alekhine suspicious. On top of that, Correira had also extracted the promise of a game from him. He'd like to see how the conceited egotist would get along in front of a chessboard. Luckily, he would be tied up with the journalist from the *Diário de Lisboa* for most of the following day.

At that moment, he remembered the envelope that had been left at his door. He emptied the contents onto the table: items clipped from various foreign newspapers, *Le Figaro*, *The Times*, *The Washington Post* . . . This time he began to examine them carefully. All, without exception, had to do with the Nuremberg trial, which had begun in November and was still under way. Among them was a full-page article that featured a photograph of the Nazi leaders in court. In an attempt to capture the entire long row of the accused in his lens, the photographer had shot the scene from a lateral angle. In the foreground, Alekhine recognized Hermann Göring, with his bon-vivant air, followed by the grim Rudolf Hess, the impeccable von Ribbentrop . . . Seen in perspective, the faces of the accused gradually got smaller and, partly because of the print grain, became difficult to make out. The strange thing was that one of the faces toward the back of the line had been circled with a red pencil. Though it seemed familiar to him, he could not identify it: it was merely a dark spot with a few white flecks. So who was the man? And who had drawn that circle around his face?

These questions, to which he could find no answer, were making his head spin. He tried to distract himself by thinking about the following day's interview with the journalist.

That night, he awakened from a nightmare that kept him from falling back asleep. He saw himself dead, lying on a dissection table; from his slashed belly, Correira was extracting handfuls of chess Pawns that were then piled on a steel counter with a deafening clang.

As soon as he opened his eyes, the blurred contours of the face of the man at the end of the row of accused became clear—and suddenly he recognized him.

■

IT WAS A day in late September, still summerlike, nature in its glory, oaks and chestnut trees just barely tinged with gold. He and his wife, Grace, were riding in the back of a Daimler convertible; the Reichsminister's personal chauffeur had come to pick them up at the Potsdam station. Grace was ecstatic at the sight of the fields that flew by, swaying like the surface of a choppy sea. Then the car turned onto a dirt road, at the end of which stood a farmhouse, barely visible, surrounded by a dense oak wood. As the car drew closer, they saw a structure with a slate roof, three gables, and white walls, on which roses climbed.

Affable and smiling, Hans Frank was waiting for them at the gate, wearing knee-high leather boots and a green woven jacket. He apologized for not being able to shake their hands, since he had just returned from hunting. It was Frau Brigitte who ushered them into the house and offered them a cool drink. And then there he was, shortly thereafter, the master of the house, reappearing all spruced up and refreshed, with a faint hint of cologne. He wore a pair of black trousers, cinched at the waist by a wide belt, and an immaculate white shirt of batiste fabric. His dark hair, slicked back, emphasized the receding hairline, but the obstinate widow's peak gave him a Latin look, like a seducer, a gaucho, or a tango dancer—so that it was almost startling to hear him speak German. It seemed impossible that the fate of Poland should be in the hands of this man, impossible to believe that he had committed all the atrocities that were attributed to him. He liked to alternate a few peaceful days in the silence of the countryside with his demanding official duties, he told them as he led them on a tour of the house: a stark interior, dark furniture, bookshelves, bronze statues, still lifes by Dutch masters on the walls.

There were other guests, also chess players: Sämisch, Richter and his wife, and Post, whose arrival had been announced. In short, the best of the German chess world. In the following days, while Grace was occupied painting Frau Brigitte's portrait, they spent their time playing chess in the shade of an oak tree. Game after game. All in consultation: Frank, Richter, and Sämisch against him, so that the responsibilities were shared, the weight of defeat eased.

Alekhine found playing outdoors at that country residence relaxing. But was it possible to dance the polka in the middle of hell? Caged in a large aviary, not far enough away from the house so that you couldn't hear its piercing shriek, was a peacock. In Russia the bird was said to bring bad luck, but its grating cry only reminded him of the ambiguous position in which he had landed. Yet he continued staying there, in the home of that patron of the arts, was gratified to be part of his court, eating the man's food, drinking his beer, laughing at his jokes, and, in chess, trying not to play his best, curbing his aggression: often he settled for a draw, since Frank couldn't stand losing, not even to him, the world champion. Merely commenting on some of his games, you had to be careful not to wound his vanity. Frank didn't take criticism well; it was clear from the way his whole body stiffened. Pointing out the flaw in what he thought was a brilliant sacrifice was enough to make him deeply despondent. Often, during the course of a match, Alekhine saw him withdraw from the game, simply staring at the board for some moments, as if to read his future there; at such times, the master would wonder what shadows were gathering, menacingly, before the man's eyes.

IX.

THE FOLLOWING MORNING, at precisely ten o'clock, he entered the
lobby. Except for a slight swelling of his eyelids, nothing hinted
at Alekhine's troubled night. He was met by a petite woman, long
hair drawn back in a ponytail, her dark eyes revealing a certain
nervousness.

After introducing herself with a handshake that was quite strong
for a woman of her size, Teresa Ocampo quickly led him to an out-of-
the-way corner of the reading room. A photographer, who was waiting with his camera already set up on a tripod, asked him to sit in an
armchair positioned in a well-lighted spot in front of the window.

On a low table beside the chair was a chessboard, its pieces scattered. A photo with a chessboard was a must. He could arrange the pieces as he thought best. Alekhine promptly recomposed the same position he'd been analyzing for some time, but soon realized that an expert would have no difficulty in reconstructing the game once the photo appeared in print—he was in danger of revealing his intentions to his opponent. He therefore changed the arrangement of the pieces, choosing a neutral position, betraying no obvious objectives; after this, he submitted to the photographer's requests. Alekhine managed to perform well before the lens, rather than facing it passively: in his youth, he had in fact attempted a career in film acting.

When the photo session was over, he ordered drinks for everyone, requesting a double *conhaque* for himself. With the sum sent to him by Lupi he could afford it, but Ocampo protested, as if it offended her professional dignity: everything would be charged to the newspaper. Soon afterward, the waiter returned with the drinks and a trayful of miniature sandwiches of prosciutto and butter. The chessboard was replaced by a monumental tape recorder, the microphone placed at the proper distance. Ocampo insisted on doing a test, and asked him to speak a few words so they could adjust the sound.

"Aleksandr Aleksandrovich Alekhin, world chess champion," he offered, pronouncing the words with a certain pomposity.

The tape was rewound. Alekhine heard his own voice replayed, cold, metallic, with an occasional foray into the high-C range, which lent it a tone of unyielding determination.

With a glass of cognac in his hand, he felt completely at ease. He took a sip. A plant wilted by drought wouldn't have reacted differently to a first drop of rain. It had been weeks since he'd tasted anything stronger than wine. A beneficent wave of warmth spread through his body. He lit a cigarette. Now he felt ready to answer any questions.

Teresa Ocampo had sat down in front of him, holding a thick notepad on her knees.

"Dr. Alekhine, I want to inform you that this interview, besides appearing in the *Diário de Lisboa*, will also be published in other newspapers, including foreign ones, as well as in some women's magazines. You have many female admirers who perhaps do not play chess, but who are very interested in your love life. I will therefore begin by asking you a few questions about your private life, which, if you choose, you may refuse to answer."

"All right," he agreed, getting comfortable.

"Dr. Alekhine, you are currently married. Your wife, Grace, however, is not here with you."

"My wife was supposed to join me, but in the end she was denied a visa. I haven't seen her in a year. At the present time she is in France, where she is trying to regain possession of all her confiscated properties, particularly the *châtellenie* of Saint-Aubin-le-Cauf, in Normandy, the family castle, which, during the war, had become the private residence and headquarters of a Nazi official."

"Can you tell us how you met her?"

"I met her in '33, in Tokyo, where I had been invited to take part in a simultaneous exhibition. In conjunction with my performance, several lower-category tournaments were also held. Grace won the women's match, and as a prize was given one of my books, *On the Road to the World Championship*, which at the end she asked me to autograph. I remember it perfectly: in the midst of a crowd of admirers I noticed a woman who was standing aside, waiting for a space to open up so she could approach me. She was clutching my book to her chest as if it were the most precious thing in the world. Her devotion won me over immediately. The following year, in the spring, we were married in Villefranche-sur-Mer, near Nice."

"The fact that your wife was more than ten years older than you was not an obstacle."

"Certainly not," he hastened to respond. "Grace is a woman who is ageless, a cultivated artist. At that time, she was highly regarded in art circles, both as a painter—Jack London commissioned a portrait from her—and as a theatrical-set designer. She was, and still is, a woman of great allure, who by no means shows her age."

"And she was also a very wealthy woman."

Alekhine made an almost imperceptible gesture of annoyance. "I know very well what you're alluding to. They always said that about me, that I seduced women for their money, but I assure you that I didn't give a damn about her assets. I was the world champion, and money was raining down on me. My years at Grace's side were happy ones. We were always traveling. I exhibited in simultaneous blindfold matches, or took part in the most important tournaments, while she played in lower-level matches. And just a couple of years ago, Grace won the women's championship in Paris."

"So it was chess that kept you together."

"Rather, an affinity of tastes, I would say, of ideals. And even a love of cats."

"Cats?"

"We had six of them roaming around the house," he said, smiling, "and sometimes we even brought some of them along on our trips."

"Did you play chess together often?"

"Oh, indeed. I was trying to hone her game, but she, too, with her great intuition, suggested a good variation or two for my own."

"Now, though, you are about to divorce."

Before answering, Alekhine held up his glass, which, in the meantime, almost without his realizing it, had been drained; he motioned the waiter to bring him another.

"It wasn't boredom that caused us to separate, though it often becomes a problem after a certain number of years of marriage. Inadvertently, we grew apart, we lost our way, much as you can lose your way on a dark night. Yet, in the letter in which Grace asked me for a divorce—a letter that I cling to and still reread—her words are those of a declaration of love. In those pages she retraces our past life

68

together, evoking the most beautiful memories. Every sentence exudes tenderness, understanding, but also profound compassion for the fate to which I am doomed."

The journalist seemed rather surprised at this.

"At a time when you are making such a strong comeback, Dr. Alekhine, here you are presenting your future in a tragic light."

"Tragic like the fate of so many artists."

"Why tragic?"

"Fundamental to the talent of men of genius is always some sort of a-priori condemnation."

"I'm not sure what you are referring to."

"It's as if, having become heir to a considerable fortune, the suspicion were to arise that the inherited legacy resulted from ancestral theft and murder. Talent likewise often appears to be an asset acquired at the expense of others, who demand its return by clamoring loudly for the appropriator's head."

Miss Ocampo now seemed to realize that she was allowing too much room for digressions, and proposed a short break. The photographer took advantage of this to shoot a few more photos of Alekhine standing beside the window that overlooked the park. The waiter, meanwhile, had served him another glass of *conhaque*, which, for the moment, he refrained from touching. The diagnosis the doctor had given him echoed in his mind, a grim reminder: if he wanted to remain world champion, he needed to enforce a period of complete sobriety. He had already done so in the past and was prepared to do it again; even though this was not really the best time to start the regimen.

After checking the list of points on her notepad, Miss Ocampo resumed her questioning.

"Dr. Alekhine, forgive me for dwelling on your romantic relationships, but there are hordes of curious admirers who want to know everything about you. This is your fourth marriage, and once again it's ending in divorce. Can you tell us something about your previous wives?"

Alekhine always felt uncomfortable when, instead of chess, he had to talk about his marital affairs.

"You first married the Baroness von Severgin, is that right?"

■

SHE WAS A friend of his mother's. The wife of an elderly Moscow land-owner, she was a beautiful woman with fiery black eyes in those days, extremely elegant and always adorned with precious jewelry, which, against her dark complexion and jet-black hair, gleamed like the gilt coverings of certain icons tarnished by the perpetual smoke of candles. She, too, like his mother, called him Tisha. He was bewitched by her: a single word from her was enough to make him blush. Aware of the power she exerted over him, the baroness seemed to enjoy teasing him, albeit gently. She was curious to know everything about him: she inquired about his progress in school and at chess, and sometimes asked him more intimate questions, just for the sake of holding his attention. "One day, you must teach me your wonderful game," she told him, holding him closely to her and sending him into ecstasies with her smile. "Will you pour me some more tea, Tisha?" she would ask then, bending down to him and thus giving him an opportunity to peek at her cleavage. Her moist red lips shone no less than her eyes. And one day, passing her a napkin, he had been unable to keep from brushing that soft, inviting breast with the back of his hand. Not at all bothered by his audacity, the baroness had laughed, and in those dark, somnolent, glistening eyes, Tisha read a promise. A promise that she would keep just a few years later.

He had only recently cast off his military-school uniform to enroll in the Faculty of Law, though in Moscow chess circles he was already a celebrity. One day, the baroness invited him to her home on the pretext of wanting to learn the game. It was the first time he'd been in her small palazzo, which faced Pyatnitskaya Street. Since she'd been widowed, the baroness lived alone. She was said to be surrounded by dozens of admirers, not counting those who had died in duels on her account.

An elderly maid came to open the door and led Alekhine up to the baroness's apartments; here she left him alone, thus giving him time to look around. Everything was arranged in a contrived display of disorder. It looked as though a series of decorators, dressmakers, bric-a-brac vendors, and art dealers had, in an attempt to persuade her to buy, scattered samples of their wares all around, waiting for her to make her decision. Lying on a row of chairs, its entire length unfolded, was a tapestry depicting a hunting scene; damask fabrics, brocades, and silks occupied every available inch of space; and there were numerous paintings as well, some on the floor leaning against the walls, others balanced precariously on the arms of chairs; among the latter, Alekhine recognized several landscapes by Shishkin and Polenov. His attention was soon drawn to a table on which a precious onyx chessboard was prominently placed. The figurines, superbly carved in ivory and red coral, were in the archaic Slavic style: a dome topped each Rook, the Bishops wore double-pointed tiaras on their heads, and crowns encircled the heads of the sovereigns, the King's culminating in a cross. The skilled carver had saved the best for the Knight's horses, however: with their dilated nostrils and wind-tossed manes, they seemed to be racing at a gallop.

"Do you like my chessboard, Tisha?"

He jumped. The baroness had come up behind him without making a sound. She wore a lavish dressing gown, edged with ostrich feathers.

"Yes, of course, it's very beautiful."

"I bought it just for you. Sit down and show me what is so extraordinary about this game that you display such passion for."

He hated playing on those artistic, purely decorative chess-boards; what's more, he felt ill-equipped for the task ahead: teaching the first moves to a beginner requires a patience that he did not possess. Still, he would do his best, even though he had the feeling that every concept, every explanation would fall on deaf ears—and the baroness, indeed, proved inattentive. She kept staring at him, and only occasionally pretended to concentrate, solely to please him. As he imagined, she was more interested in him than in chess. He felt flattered by her attentions, yet he was sorry to see her so indifferent to the game. Her jittery hands were adorned with massive gold rings set with precious stones. Those same hands would soon explore every inch of his body.

Although he had tried numerous times to recall the route by which they had transitioned from the chessboard to the bedroom, that passage had been erased from his memory. He had only a vague recollection—little more than a glimmer—of her taking him by the arm and luring him on with a promise to show him something, leading him down a long corridor, at the end of which a door had been left open. And then a much sharper image of himself lying on a four-poster bed, wearing only his shirt, unable to move under her weight. The same sensation he had sometimes had as a child when, waking in the middle of the night, he found himself overpowered by the *domovoi*, crushing his chest and taking his breath away along with any remaining strength.

Everything that for years had fueled his most daring fantasies was concluded in a flash, and in a way that was quite different from what he had imagined, leaving him a residue of disappointment and bitterness. It was the first time he'd been with a woman, and the feeling was similar to that of a stinging defeat at the board. Leaving that house, he promised himself never to return; instead, not even a week went by before he was again knocking at the baroness's door. And from then on the meetings with her became a regular date: he visited her every week, on Tuesdays and Sundays, and each time he became bolder, more demanding. Brought up in the traditional Christian faith, he felt the burden of sin weigh heavily on him, though at the same time he was proud to have passed into adulthood and to be able to compete, if he wished, with the most licentious libertines. But when desire had run its course and he had satisfied every curiosity, he began to feel a growing revulsion for the baroness, and started skipping their meetings. This she would not tolerate and often their occasional encounters now turned into furious arguments. Finally, when the baroness announced to him that she was pregnant, he decided to break off their relations entirely: he couldn't stand the fact that growing within her was living proof of their union.

X.

"D R. ALEKHINE, WOULD you perhaps prefer not to answer?"
The reporter was staring at him quizzically.

"Yes," he confirmed, "my first wife was the Baroness von Severgin.
It was, however, a shotgun wedding. We'd had a daughter, Valentina,
you see, after an affair that occurred several years earlier . . ."

"At that time you were still a cadet."

"Not exactly. I was very young, twenty years old, attending university, and found myself already the father of a child. Although Moscow
was hardly a provincial village, rumors had begun to spread. Fortu-
nately, the baroness's turbulent love life allowed for other suppositions. Only my mother knew the truth, and she made me swear that I

would right my wrong. The marriage, however, could only be offici-
ated eight years later, when the war had ended, and immediately after
the wedding my wife left Russia and moved to Austria with the child.
Since that time, despite having written to her many times, I've never
heard another word from her, nor have I had any news of her or
my daughter."

"And you never felt a desire to see them again?"

In response to that question Alekhine remained impassive. "Since
I received no reply to my letters, I felt that a visit from me wouldn't be
welcome."

"There is also another child, from your second marriage . . ."

"Yes, and he bears my name: Aleksandr Aleksandrovich Alekhin.
I am on good terms with him. We've met several times, and we write
often. Aleksandr lives in Düsseldorf, and is a metallurgical engineer.
He was the offspring of my marriage to Anneliese Rüegg, a Swiss
journalist whom I met in Germany when I was an interpreter for the
Comintern. It was thanks to her that I was able to emigrate from my
beloved Russia, by then in the hands of the Bolsheviks. But that marriage, too, failed. She, after a few years, could no longer put up with
my way of life."

The reporter flipped through the sheets in her hand.

"And then there was Nadezhda Fabritskaya."

■

SHE HAD BEEN his third wife, the widow of a tsarist general and former
admiral, always so bedecked with jewels that she earned the nickname
"Frau Tannenbaum." He remembered her haughty air, her single
arched eyebrow, her wrinkled nose forever thrust into a scented handkerchief, her forever being on the verge of swooning over the slightest thing, always so tightly cinched in her whalebone *guêpière*, propped
up by stiff cretonne fabrics, crowned with reddish hairpieces that

resembled a mountainous sugarloaf. Out of courtesy, it had never crossed his mind to ask her age; he could only guess it by the fact that Guendalina, her only child, was actually older than he was. For that matter, he had never even been able to discover what lay concealed beneath that walking baldachin, nor had he ever had any desire to inquire too closely. Fortunately for him, they slept in separate rooms, and their rare moments of intimacy—she was more and more terrified by microbes—were consummated in total darkness. He had never told anyone that the marriage had, in reality, been the result of a ridiculous misunderstanding, entirely worthy of a vaudeville comedy.

With the title of world champion had come success and prosperity, and if anything was still lacking it was simply a stable place to which to return from his itinerant life. Tired by then of always having to live in a hotel, Alekhine had actually started thinking about making a good match and raising a family. At that time his presence was highly sought after in Parisian drawing rooms, and Fabritskaya had welcomed him to her beautiful apartment, situated in one of the most elegant neighborhoods of Paris. And when she had invited him to her home for the first time, on the occasion of one of the many musical matinées she hosted, he had also met the daughter, a drab, gangling woman, shy to the point of not being able to utter a word in the presence of a man. No wonder she was still unmarried—but he might as well make an attempt, he thought. During his increasingly persistent visits to their home, he saw, however, that it was impossible to be alone with the daughter—the mother was unfailingly present. As he recounted his travels and adventures, the young woman always seemed uncomfortable, her eyes continually averted, as if afraid of meeting his, whereas Nadezhda followed his stories with growing interest. Without being aware of it, therefore, he was courting the wrong person. The consequences were as unforeseeable as they were grotesque. Having decided to ask for Guendalina's hand, he showed up at the door one day with a large bouquet of roses and asked Nadezhda if he might speak to her in private. Instead of going straight to the point, he declared with some confusion that his lovesick heart had led him to that state and had given him no peace since he entered her house for the first time. Nadezhda misunderstood and, turning pale, confessed in a whisper, *"Oh, Alexandre, je t'aime trop,"* before falling into his arms in a swoon.

Thus, albeit in a completely unexpected way, he managed to get what he wanted: in the end, rather than the mummified Guendalina, the mother was indeed preferable. If he had any regrets, they were only for the way he had treated her, venting his bad moods, anger, and frustrations on her, and making her the chosen victim of all his excesses. Surely, after putting up with his tyranny for years, Nadezhda had won herself a place in heaven.

■

"I WOULD RATHER not talk about that saintly woman," Alekhine pleaded.

"Of course."

Miss Ocampo nervously consulted the pages of her notepad, skipping a few points. Finally, she found a place to resume.

"You have led quite an eventful life. You were imprisoned more than once for political reasons."

"Yes, that is correct. The first time was in Germany, in Mannheim, where a major international tournament was being held. I was ahead by nine wins, one loss, and one draw. Although there were still a few rounds to play, my lead was unbridgeable and my victory assured. Suddenly, the tournament was suspended."

"And the reason for the suspension?"

"A minor diplomatic incident, let's say: Germany had declared war on Russia. In addition to myself, there were at least eleven other Russian players participating in the tournament, so you can imagine the authorities' embarrassment: technically, we were prisoners of war. We remained in custody for a few days. I was the last to be freed, because, while searching through my personal belongings, they found a photo of me in my cadet outfit, which some idiot mistook for an army uniform. Eventually, however, the misunderstanding was cleared up, and they decided to transport us to Baden-Baden, to await repatriation. We were sure we had escaped the worst, but we were wrong. During the train trip, some of us passed the time playing chess. A watchful conductor found some score sheets we had used to jot down our moves. He thought they were some sort of secret code. At the Ramstadt station, he alerted the police, who slammed us all back in prison. For about twenty days, I was locked in a cell with Bogolyubov. We passed the time playing blindfold, one game after another. Then they separated us, and put me in solitary confinement.

"Ultimately, as an alternative to prison, our only option was to enlist in the German army. I had no physical defects and was in perfect health. Luckily for me, the doctor assigned to examine me was an admirer of mine, and declared me unfit for military service 'due to suspected mental disorder.' Considering me therefore completely harmless, they eased their surveillance of me, and although the competition had been suspended, I was granted the sum of eleven hundred marks as the undisputed winner of the tournament. I used part of that money to help some of my fellow unfortunates and to procure false papers for myself. It was very risky: had they caught me, I would have immediately been sent before a firing squad. But once again I was lucky, and managed to leave the country.

"Crossing through Switzerland, I reached Genoa. There I embarked on a Russian ship, which, before bringing me back home, sailed around half of Europe: England, Sweden, Finland . . . At each port of call, I took the opportunity to play in some simultaneous matches. I arrived in St. Petersburg at the end of October, and from there I finally reached Moscow."

Miss Ocampo seemed quite impressed by his story. Alekhine

noticed this and felt a kind of inner gratification, which turned into genuine self-satisfaction when she asked him: "Was there perhaps another time when your celebrity was of help to you in a difficult situation?"

"Oh yes, I remember clearly one day when, together with Chess, I managed to cross the Polish border without a passport. I simply said that I was the world chess champion and that I had no need of a passport. The border guards were bewildered. They whispered together for a while, then went into the gatehouse to make some phone calls. Eventually, an officer appeared and, after studying my face closely, ordered them to let me through."

"And who was Chess?"

"He was my beloved Siamese cat. I always took him with me, even to the tournaments. The regulations did not prohibit it, maybe because no one had ever thought it possible that a chess player might bring along his cat. But Chess was a quiet little creature; he strolled among the tables and didn't bother anyone. When he sensed that I was in trouble, he would leap on my knees and encourage me by purring."

The journalist pressed him: "Are there any other such incidents that come to mind?"

"Well, there was an episode in which—I still can't explain how—the game actually saved my life."

"Tell me about it."

"I was in Odessa, just after the Revolution. I was staying in a hotel room that had been previously occupied by a British officer. He had left some compromising documents in a drawer, which were found during a search by the Cheka, the Russian secret police. My protestations of innocence were of no use. I was accused of espionage and sentenced to death by firing squad. On the eve of my execution, two guards entered my cell. One of the two was carrying a chessboard under his arm. Behind them, Trotsky himself appeared, and invited me to play a game. I was astonished. But I had no choice but to accept. We began to play. Meanwhile, I kept wondering what I should do. Should I indulge him with a draw? Win by a narrow margin? Crush him like a bug? Given that the firing squad awaited me at dawn the following day, I thought I might as well go out on a high note, so I did not spare him—I showed him no mercy. I even took the satisfaction of announcing a forced checkmate in seven moves. At the end of the match, I thought I saw a bare hint of a smile on that inscrutable face. I expected him to react, to say something; but no, he merely stood, picked up the chessboard, and walked out of my cell without a single word. The next morning, at the first light of dawn, I heard gunshots begin at regular intervals, coming from the prison's inner yard. By the time the guards arrived, I was prepared to die. They escorted me to the end of a long corridor, but then, at the last moment, rather than shoving me into the bloodbath, they opened the prison door for me and told me that I was free to leave."

The journalist must have been satisfied by those stories, because she now switched to a completely different topic: "Dr. Alekhine, after nine years of unchallenged supremacy, you will shortly have to defend your title against a leading exponent of Soviet chess. It will be an awkward situation, don't you think?"

"If the world changes, it is certainly through no fault of chess, nor can chess be influenced by revolutions and wars," he replied cautiously. "My adversary is primarily an adversary at the chessboard, certainly not in life, nor as regards political ideals."

"I meant: awkward for the Soviets," she clarified.

Alekhine shrugged slightly.

"It was the Moscow club that put together the necessary sum, it is they who are anxious to recover the title to flaunt it to the world; besides, the match will take place in England, not in the Soviet Union."

"Regardless, in their eyes you remain a dissident, a traitor."

At those words, he reached for the glass that he had left untouched on a small table beside him, and drained it in one gulp. "Because of some of my statements against the new regime, my brother, Aleksei, who remained in Russia and espoused their cause, publicly renounced me and my ideas—or, rather, he was forced to do so. His loyalty was repaid, two years later, with murder." His voice almost cracked, but he quickly regained control. "The long arm of the regime, unable to reach me, decided to punish me by brutally killing my beloved brother."

"And you never feared that you might suffer the same fate?"

"You mean being killed?"

The journalist nodded.

He hesitated a moment, then: "Perhaps, yes, now and then, the thought's occurred to me."

"After all," Ocampo said, a little heavy-handedly, "Trotsky himself, despite taking refuge in Mexico, was ultimately hit by a hired assassin."

"I took my precautions."

For a time, Alekhine was silent. In fact, he knew very well that it was not strictly necessary for a victim to be close to his murderer, that there was no place in the world where one could be assured of finding a completely secure refuge. A well-trained hit man could strike even in broad daylight and in the midst of a crowd.

Clearing her throat, the reporter called him back to the present. She must have realized that, at this rate, she was in danger of seeing the interview go up in smoke, because she suddenly brought the conversation back to chess.

"Dr. Alekhine, there's a twenty-year age difference between you and your challenger."

"Nineteen," he corrected her, slightly irritated.

"All right, nineteen. Don't you think that might pose a disadvantage for you?"

"If you are alluding to physical endurance, keep in mind that it is not the hours spent at the board that tire me. If anything, it's the waiting, the delays, the intervals between one match and another. The board for me is like a magnet: it attracts me irresistibly and charges me with renewed energy. When I play, I am immersed in my world. It's only there that I feel alive . . . only there that I can find a life apart from this miserable, contradictory one."

"As we read in your book, you envisioned your path to the title from the time you were still quite young and were just beginning to emerge in the chess world. Even then you had set yourself a specific goal."

Alekhine knew that sooner or later he would have to do it, so he decided to be the first to broach the subject and, not without some effort, spoke that detestable name.

"Capablanca was the man to beat. At that time, he was the most formidable. They called him 'the machine built to win.' But I studied his matches closely, and I did not feel he was unbeatable. There were few players able to stand up to him, it's true: Lasker, who had just lost the title, did not even consider it. And Rubinstein didn't have the strength of character. But, all things considered, I was the ideal challenger."

"It was an arduous undertaking."

"Arduous?" he echoed her. "I'd say downright hellish. And I am not referring only to the superhuman stress to which I was subjected, but to the physical suffering as well. Besides the unbearable heat and the attacks of dysentery, during the course of the third game I was overcome by intense neuralgia, caused by an infection in my upper dental arch, which required me to undergo painful dental treatments during the match. It became necessary to extract six teeth. What was left in my mouth was comparable to the worst array of Pawns imaginable. Until, later on, a skilled dentist . . ." With his index finger, he raised his lip to expose prostheses made of gold and platinum.

"But once the title was in your hands," Ocampo ventured, "you took care not to give him a rematch. You preferred to compete with less aggressive opponents, such as Bogolyubov."

"I only insisted that certain conditions be met," Alekhine said curtly, "such as the amount of the pot and the choice of venue. My opponent was accustomed to torrid climates, but I prefer temperate ones. It was within my rights to be able to choose. In any case, due to the crisis of '29, Capablanca was never able to put together the sum of money required to get his chance."

"And yet he was considered the only player capable of taking the title from you."

"By that time, his game had visibly deteriorated. Capablanca was lazy—I don't really think he was all that eager to play anymore. He relied on his positional sense; he avoided risks and complications and became entirely predictable. Lasker himself, in an interview given after his defeat, affirmed that Capablanca's game was based on fundamental rules, and that he very rarely made an unexpected move—he guided the pieces like a shepherd guiding his flock, satisfied to lead only one to the pen, and whatever small advantage he gained in that way, he managed to maintain until the end. If you analyze his games closely, you discover quite a few weak moves, if not actual errors, and even in his endgames he was not exactly the 'prodigy' that many thought he was. Drawing a comparison with music, he composed charming minuets, whereas I aspired to create majestic symphonies."

"You were friends, in your youth . . ."

"You can be friends in life and adversaries at the chessboard."

"You two, however, became adversaries in life as well."

"When there are big gains at stake, it can happen."

"In the end, you were defeated by Max Euwe."

Alekhine waved a hand, as if this wasn't even worth talking about.

"A mere setback. Euwe was a mathematician, a calculator, certainly nowhere near Capablanca's strength. Recapturing the title two years later was child's play."

Ocampo allowed herself a brief pause. It was time to change the subject again.

"Dr. Alekhine, are you in Portugal as an exile or as a political refugee?"

"I would rather not answer."

"Is it true that you were summoned several times by the Allied Control Commission to clarify your position?"

"I have never been summoned," he snapped, irritated. "And, furthermore, I really don't know what there would be to clarify. Should I perhaps have explained that I played chess wherever it was still possible to do so?"

"Is it true that you and your wife were about to emigrate to the United States, but were denied an entry visa?"

"No, that is false. It was our decision to remain in Europe."

"Some insinuate that you were unable to obtain a visa because of several pro-Nazi articles."

Alekhine ordered his third glass. He could feel his anger mounting. His vanity, however, got the upper hand, and allowed him to maintain his self-control. He was the center of attention for the international press and had to be able to remain composed. He smiled pleasantly, crossed his legs, and let his body sink back against the chair as he fumbled in his pocket for some cigarettes. That posture, in front of a chessboard, would have been an inauspicious portent for his opponent.

"My dear Miss Ocampo," he said, with all the amiability he could rally, "I have undergone a number of harsh interrogations in my life. All of them seem quite mild, in retrospect, compared with yours."

The woman blushed violently at first, then, in an alarming transition, turned almost instantly pale. She bent forward. Was she about to pass out? No, she was only turning off the tape recorder. She seemed contrite about having gone too far.

"I'm sorry to have touched upon such sensitive matters. If you like, I can erase whatever you think is inappropriate from the tape."

"I have nothing to hide. Everything I told you is the truth," Alekhine replied with a half-smile.

The photographer, seeing him smile for the first time, insisted on taking a few more shots of him, but was unable to coax out more than a sardonic grin.

Being able to talk with the tape recorder off restored Alekhine's good humor. As if seeking forgiveness, Ocampo now kept strictly to the topic of chess.

"Is it true that chess can also lead to madness?"

Alekhine regarded her with a kind of indulgent condescension.

"You see, my dear lady, not many laymen are aware that, to fully appreciate the complexity of this magnificent art form, one must also have a considerable knowledge. To acquire this knowledge, one must devote oneself exclusively to chess from a young age, which means giving up a balanced development of the mind. So, yes, I do believe that focusing on a single object of interest to the exclusion of all else can certainly lead to insanity."

"Could you name some of the players to whom this happened?"

"There are several examples, but one individual whom I knew personally: Akiba Rubinstein, an Eastern Jew. His most significant achievement was to share first prize with Emanuel Lasker in St. Petersburg in 1909. A memorable tournament, in which I myself participated, at just sixteen. After another few years of triumph, he began an imperceptible downward slide. He never stopped studying, but it was evident that he was putting excessive strain on a brain that, though talented at chess, was rather mediocre. Undoubtedly, in the last ten years of his endeavors, Rubinstein still played some good games, but his mental disorder became more and more apparent. During tournaments, he used to run away from the board—literally—after each move he made, taking refuge in a corner of the room and resuming his place only when the other player had responded to his move. He did this— he explained—so as not to be subject to the malign influence of his opponent's ego. Currently, Rubinstein lives somewhere in Belgium, but he hasn't participated in a tournament in years."

"So, then, do you have other passions besides chess?"

"Oh yes. I'm interested in music, painting, languages, literature. I also love horseback riding and table tennis—an activity that relaxes me."

"Over the course of your career, is there one memory that stands out?"

"When I won the title, beating Capablanca with a three-point lead, I was carried in triumph through the streets of Buenos Aires. I was acclaimed by more than ten thousand people."

"And among all the prizes you have received, which was the one you felt most gratified by?"

"When I won the national tournament at age sixteen, the tsar himself gave me a precious Sèvres vase adorned with the imperial eagle. In 1921, I was allowed to take it out of Russia, and since that time, though it's extremely fragile, I have always brought it along with me wherever I lived. Only once did I happen to forget it: it was left in Paris, at my wife's home, when we moved. For months and months, I lived in anguish that it might suffer some damage. On my return, I found it in the midst of some worthless junk that had been piled up in the cellar. When I saw the state the case was in, my blood froze. Fortunately, the vase itself was still intact. There was only a tiny chip on the rim, which I took pains to have repaired in Lisbon by a master ceramicist. At a high cost, but it was well worth it."

The conversation ended at the bar, where Alekhine allowed himself yet another glass. The photographer took his picture again as he drank.

"IS THERE ANYTHING you regret about your past?" Ocampo asked.

"Many things. Too many. But I prefer to keep them to myself."

"And what do you miss most?"

"My beloved Russia," he replied without hesitation.

Before leaving, the journalist handed him an envelope, which he slipped into his pocket with studied indifference. Not for anything in the world would he let her or anyone else know how much he needed that money.

XI.

THERE, IT'S STARTING again. The thirsty beast is never satisfied with one little drink. Hard to keep it in check. Maybe at first it wants you to think that a sip or two will make you feel good, that a shot of *conhaque* is all you need to loosen your tongue and make you more mellow and congenial. After all, the finest company is always found around the cask; it doesn't matter whether you are in an infamous dive or a luxury hotel. In Paris, Alekhine had drunk while rubbing shoulders with Jack London, Ian Fleming, Marcel Duchamp, and even Rudyard Kipling, when the latter had slipped the net of his despotic wife, who measured out his whiskey with a dropper. And at the Hollywood Chess Club, where he had been invited by Douglas

Fairbanks, Jr., to perform in a simultaneous match, Alekhine had downed several martinis along with Humphrey Bogart and Lauren Bacall—they, too, chess enthusiasts. The best people, the most brilliant and insightful, are found at the bar, one foot resting on the rail, and it's truly a pity that, the following morning, you wake up without the slightest recollection of some of them. Still, those moments are full of poetry, of prophetic vision, of sublime profundity. You'll see: after your first sip, the world will go back to shining in all its splendor, or so says the voice of that devious, craving monster who darts between your brain and your stomach, as slippery as an eel.

■

"BRING ME ANOTHER, and make it a double!" he called to the bartender. "Let's drink to Europe, which has been reduced to ashes, but which will soon rise again, like the phoenix. The Nazis are on the run—once they were hunters, now they've become the prey. What future awaits me in this new world? *Oh, mein Gott, wie soll ich das alles nur aushalten?* How will I ever bear it?"

■

KNOWING SEVERAL LANGUAGES, he often switched from one to another, according to the mood of the moment, and in general, in his private ruminations, he expressed himself in German. The barman, who didn't understand a single word of Alekhine's monologue, merely smiled at him and refilled his glass to the brim.

Chess and alcohol had grown up with him together, like a pair of mismatched traveling companions. At home, alcohol was never lacking: his father, who lived most of the year in France, would send back cases of champagne and cognac. The glass panes of the credenzas displayed nothing but bottles, all within easy reach, and his mother would waft through the house, always somewhat unsteady, always pleasantly tipsy. It was during his first colossal drinking spree, while on leave with the cadets, that he had learned of his ability to hold his liquor better than his comrades, and he had been quite proud of this. While some struggled to stay on their feet, he could still walk a straight line, and when others burst into bawdy songs, he maintained a composure and a lucidity that gave him a new sense of omnipotence.

Without realizing it, however, he had entered an endless vortex. Since he was a boy, he'd been accustomed to seeing his mother in a stupor, lying on a chaise longue, a glass still clutched in her fingers; once, he'd even found her unconscious on the floor, her hand cut by glass fragments. Would he end up like his mother, who had died an alcoholic? He learned soon enough that he could not control himself where alcohol was concerned. By then, a state of acceptable euphoria was no longer enough for him. The fire that he felt burning inside required more and more fuel each day, and the greater the stack of wood he burned, the higher the heaps of ashes grew. Alcohol raised him up to dizzying heights, only to plunge him into a bottomless sea.

On some official occasions, he'd gotten drunk enough to provoke embarrassing incidents, insulting high-ranking individuals or making rude attempts to seduce their wives. During a tournament—he could no longer remember which one—he had urinated in a pot of *Ficus benjamina*. Sometimes, after a few drinks too many, he would be overcome by anger, indignation. At those times, he no longer had respect for anything or anyone, nor was he concerned about the consequences of his behavior. During a simultaneous match on forty chessboards in occupied Paris, he realized, when play had started, that they had hastily added a place for a senior officer of the SS. He pretended not to notice initially, but as soon as he reached his turn with the intruder, he overturned the entire board on him, not at all intimidated by his uniform, and then continued the round undaunted. There were countless other times, however, when he had lost consciousness completely, eventually waking up in unfamiliar places without knowing how he had gotten there. A few years earlier, in Madrid, he had even found himself in the bed of a psychiatric hospital, for having shown—so they said—signs of mental derangement.

Drinking had had disastrous effects on his game. He had suffered his worst losses in an alcoholic haze. He still remembered the first, at age sixteen, against Romanovsky. A laughable game: with two pieces down, Alekhine was still trying to checkmate him. And then the last one, against Euwe, which had cost him the world title. After that defeat, he had managed to make a clean break. To regain the title, he'd needed to submit to a rigid discipline: he had given up alcohol entirely and had gone from forty cigarettes a day to a barely a dozen. He spent months restoring his vitality, in Baden-Baden and in Rogaška Slatina, drinking only thermal waters and taking long, strenuous hikes in the woods.

No, he would not end up like his mother. He was capable of giving up alcohol whenever he wanted.

"I'll stop drinking," he promised himself solemnly, prepared to recant in order to survive. "I'll stop drinking, but not today. Today I must celebrate. One more, the last!"

Alekhine drew the envelope with the money out of his pocket, but the barman shook his head and set the bottle in front of him.

"*A garrafa é oferecida pelo* Diário."

Alekhine glanced briefly at the sum that he'd been paid, then slipped out a bill, laid it on the counter, and with the palm of his hand pushed it toward the barman.

"*Obrigado, senhor.*"

He tucked the bottle under his arm as if it were a baguette, and left the bar. Only now did he realize that his vision was getting blurry. Crossing the lobby unsteadily, he heard the roar of an engine, and through the window saw a sports car racing up and stopping in front of the hotel, raising a cloud of dust. A couple got out and headed for the reception desk. The man was wearing a tweed jacket with leather trim; he was tall, with graying hair and a thin mustache that seemed drawn on with a ruler. She, a curly-haired little blonde, perhaps a starlet, was almost certainly American. While her companion was signing the register, the girl looked around, smiling blankly. She wore white high-heeled shoes and, under an unbuttoned trench coat, a cashmere sweater and plaid skirt. She had beautiful eyes, an intense blue. If they had any luggage, they'd left it in the car, the man carrying only a tennis racket sheathed in a canvas case, and the woman a hatbox. As they passed by Alekhine, the young woman gave him a swift glance. She was the kind of woman who looks at you just to make sure she's admired. She resembled one of those pinups that embodied the feminine ideal of young American men sent to the front, images that by now were appearing everywhere, even on drinking glasses and coffee cups, always with their skirts lifted by a mischievous puff of wind. Behind her the woman left a trail of scent that reawakened a long-dormant desire in Alekhine.

Despite his unsteadiness, he managed to drag himself to his room. But he continued to smell that perfume, to see before him that petite, exciting woman. Then, almost unaware of what he was doing, he pressed the button to call the floor attendant. The wait seemed interminable. Finally, the girl came to the door. She was still wiping her hands on a dish towel.

"*Quer alguma coisa, senhor?*" Would you like something?

"What's your name?" he asked her.

"Estela."

"Come in, Estela, come here."

The women in Estoril all looked alike: small, sturdy, with a low hairline and dark complexion. Estela was an exception: though of modest stature, she was well proportioned and had slender ankles and a high forehead. She was young, with a beautiful smile and thick, dark eyebrows that seemed to converge at the top of her nose. He was sitting on the side of his bed, but Estela showed no fear in approaching; she must have been used to such advances.

Alekhine grabbed her hand and pulled her to him. Then he began to unbutton her blue blouse.

"*Senhor . . .*" the girl protested feebly. He thought he read a note of apprehension in her eyes, as if she knew that his heart was bad. But then, meekly, she let him undo the buttons. Under the blouse she was naked. He lingered at the sight of those newly budded breasts; then his eyes followed the constellation of tiny moles that ran from her sternum down toward the dark shadow of her abdomen. For a moment the thought occurred to him that she might be pregnant, and at the same time a faint scent of cheap soap, mixed with that of cleaning detergents, triggered a revulsion that led him to push her abruptly away.

"*Senhor, não gosta de mim?*" You do not like me?

He shook his head. He took both of her hands, reddened by lye, then caressed her face and asked her to get dressed again.

"*Você é linda, mas eu estou muito bêbado,*" he said. You're beautiful, but I am too drunk.

Estela rebuttoned her blouse, pretending to pout, but she brightened when he slipped a couple of bills into her pocket.

"*Obrigada,*" the girl said, and hurried out of the room.

■

EVEN HIS DEALINGS with women were hampered by alcohol. Or why not admit that he had never had an excessive interest in them to begin with? Why not confess that at times he was satisfied to raise the skirt of a floor attendant or a maid? Some pretended to be indignant, but then they usually still submitted to those swift caresses of his, which never went very far and in the end assured them that they were satisfying a modest whim. War, poverty, hunger had made them all available, albeit in compliance with form, as with the exchange of goods acquired on the black market and discreetly sold under the table. And then there were the prostitutes, who were hardly there to judge a client's performance, provided he paid them. For him these were the preferable type of interaction, short-lived, with no complications or consequences. He had begun suffering from impotence at age forty. At times, he merely observed the clumsy stirring of that part of his body as though it were foreign, alienated from him by an immeasurable distance, only subsequently reuniting with it, so to speak, the way the meaning of a joke heard at a party only comes to you long afterward, once the party is over, when confetti and streamers cover the floor of a now empty room, prompting an uproarious, solitary laugh. Yet he'd been married four times. The first of them, he had to admit, had held a strong physical attraction for him, at least initially; but the truth is that the other three had only served as refuges. On their laps, when he was drunk, he could lay his head and weep like a baby.

XII.

SHORTLY AFTERWARD, HE left his room to knock at the adjacent door. Neumann opened it, and by Alekhine's appearance must have sensed that something was wrong, because he quickly invited him to come in.

"Dr. Alekhine, what has happened to you?"

Alekhine leaned against the doorjamb so as not to lose his balance, then, after taking a few steps, sank into an armchair. Neumann closed the door behind him.

"Do you feel ill?" Neumann persisted.

How to explain that strange, unbearable feeling: as if a blind, excruciating probe were sounding his inner depths?

"I'm fine, I'm fine. I just need you to play me something that will take me back in time . . ."

Neumann was holding a napkin, and there were still plates and dishes on his table: clearly, he had not finished his lunch. But Alekhine pretended not to notice, and the violinist accepted his bizarre request with good grace. He went to get his violin.

"What would you like to hear, Dr. Alekhine?"

"Listen, let's stop with this Dr. Alekhine!" the master burst out. "Call me Alexandre, like my friends do. Because we're friends, aren't we?" He spoke with some difficulty, feeling as though his mouth were full of cotton wool, and in his own plaintive tone he recognized the intrusiveness of a drunkard in search of human contact. There had been many times, during his binges, when he'd been carried away by similar unthinkable transports toward people he'd barely met, only to regret it later on, once he sobered up.

"Of course I'm your friend . . ." Neumann said, a bit surprised by this sudden familiarity.

"Then call me Alexandre."

"Of course . . . Alexandre."

"Thank you, David! I can call you that, can't I?"

"Of course."

"Now play something for me. It will soon be spring. I would so love to hear something tender that will bring me back to the flowering almond trees of my childhood."

Neumann appeared to run through his repertoire mentally. Finally, he began Beethoven's *Frühlingssonate*.

Alekhine listened to the opening Allegro with his eyes closed, sketching vague swirls in the air with his hand, as if he were directing an invisible orchestra. Then, during the Adagio, his face relaxed into an expression of peaceful bliss.

A LUMINOUS DAY, the garden at home, with the whole family gathered around a circular table for the taking of a keepsake photo. He was in the middle, standing, being embraced by his grandmother. On one side sat his mother, and Varvara and Aleksei completed the other side of the semicircle. Every year, in spring, when the weather was fine, the family group-photo ritual was repeated. In some of the pictures, from way back, his father even appeared.

The photographer was a small man with a gray beard who wore a tall black felt top hat. He arrived carrying all his equipment on his back, set up his tripod, and on it placed a wooden box from which something like the end of a stubby telescope protruded. When everything was ready, he stuck his head under a black cloth, ordering everyone to remain absolutely still. At the instant when the guncotton flashed, his grandmother hugged the boy even tighter; right after that Tisha heard her breathe a sigh and thank God that they'd escaped this danger.

His name was Rosenbaum, the photographer, and he was a Jew. Even then that word, *Jew*, aroused in Alekhine a certain emotion, a mixture of superstitious fear and admiration. One day, he'd asked his mother how come they weren't Jews. She laughed and explained to him that they couldn't be, simply because Jews were a different race.

A few years later, driven by curiosity, he started going to the Jewish Quarter. It was the busiest part of the city. Goldsmiths, merchants, junk dealers, sitting in front of small shops crammed with merchandise, hawked their varied wares, bringing them out to the street. They were constantly haggling over the value of each object, negotiating the price loudly; sometimes furious arguments broke out. The men were dressed in black, with wide-brimmed hats; some wore caftans, and they all sported long, tangled beards, so different from the well-trimmed ones worn by the aristocrats and bourgeoisie, and even from those of the Orthodox priests. Roaming through the multitudes were hieratic figures who seemed deep in meditation, moving their lips in interminable prayer. They prayed—so Tisha had been told—that the Messiah might come to earth and "turn the world inside out."

■

IN THE MIDDLE of that picturesque bedlam, amid the flurry of the crowd, Tisha saw numerous boys raptly playing chess. Squatting on the steps of a house or on the curb, they were so focused that nothing around them could serve as a distraction. They, too, like the adults, were dressed in black, and wore hats and long corkscrew sideburns. With his schoolboy uniform and short, closely shaved hair, Tisha stood out among them like a rara avis. Sometimes he stopped to observe a game, hoping that he might be invited to play, but he was well aware that Jews avoided goyim. Usually, his presence was tolerated, but often enough someone would gather up the board in irritation and move somewhere else, thereby letting Tisha know that he wasn't welcome. In time, going there, he would come to realize that for Jews chess was more than just a game: it was virtually a sacred rite. And in this regard he felt very much like them.

One day, at last, his patience was rewarded. One of the boys whom he often saw playing got tired of waiting for his usual opponent to show up and with a patronizing wave of his hand invited Tisha to approach. The young man started out moving the pieces with feigned indifference, perhaps thinking he would wrap up the game in a few strokes, but after a while the time he spent reflecting between one move and another lengthened considerably. Meanwhile, a knot of curious onlookers formed around them. The boy's companion also finally appeared and, finding him playing with a goy, reproached him sharply. The two argued briefly in Yiddish; then the opponent stormed off in a huff. To Tisha it seemed very strange that a simple game of chess could cause so much resentment. He stood up to leave, but the other boy urged him to continue. Tisha was flattered: evidently, this boy thought highly of his game. They resumed the match, which, after countless moves, ended in a draw. At the end, the Jewish boy gave him a knowing smile and shook his hand.

◼

THAT WAS THE first time he'd faced a Jewish chess player—it would certainly not be the last. He would endure a stinging defeat by Rubinstein in the first masters tournament in which he competed. He was eighteen years old then, and, encountering that young man, some years older than him, who was said to have abandoned his rabbinical studies to devote himself to chess, he'd had to swallow several bitter truths. Later on, he played against Nimzowitsch, Lasker, and Reshevsky, soon realizing that, in his rise to the world title, his competitors would all be Jews.

Their faces were still sharply etched in his memory: Rubinstein, dapper, with a crew cut and an upturned mustache and the vacant gaze of a man who has peered too closely into his own madness; Lasker, with his perpetually drowsy air and spiraling, hopelessly rebellious hair; Nimzowitsch, looking like a bank clerk who, behind his pincenez, is haughtily judging the insufficiency of other people's funds; Reshevsky, resembling a prematurely aged child prodigy. Often he imagined them muffled up in long black cloaks, gathered in a circle like crows around a carcass, intent on captiously interpreting chess the way they did their sacred texts.

XIII.

H E HEARD A voice calling him from a distance. When he opened his eyes, he found Neumann's face flashing before him in a stroboscopic light. He couldn't make out where he was; the walls of the room were still where they should have been, but someone, meanwhile, seemed to have moved the furniture. Alekhine looked around for his armchair and the coffee table that held his chessboard . . . He couldn't understand why they weren't in their places. Then, piece by piece, he put together the events of the day. Had he slept? He glanced at his wristwatch. It was almost five.

Neumann was urging him to get up.

"Come on, let's go outside, Alexandre, a little air will do you good."

For a moment, it seemed odd that Neumann would call him by his first name. Immediately afterward, however, he remembered that he himself had asked the violinist to do so, had insisted on it, in fact; and, all things considered, it did not displease him.

"Oh, leave me be, David. I just want to go back to my room."

"You can't go on ruining yourself . . ."

"No sermons, David, please. I wish I could be somewhere else, somewhere no one knows me. I'm getting scared—I feel as though everyone is staring at me. They all seem convinced that I have committed some kind of terrible crime, but I assure you that it's not true . . ."

"Of course, of course . . . Now, though, you could use a nice breath of fresh air. Nothing better than a brisk walk along the shore to pull yourself together. You have to be in top shape."

"Why?"

"Because you are the world champion, and will remain so. You haven't forgotten that, have you?"

"You were right to remind me of it, David," Alekhine agreed, once again letting himself be lulled by flattery.

■

SHORTLY AFTERWARD, THEY walked side by side along the beach, heading toward the lighthouse. The breeze had become stiffer. During the walk, they did not exchange a single word. But among friends, Alekhine thought, it was not strictly necessary to speak. On the way back, the golden hue of the sea had turned a blood red. Alekhine hated the light of sundown, whereas Neumann, for his part, basked in it. From time to time, the violinist stopped to climb up on a rock, entranced by the reflections on the water. Viewed from behind, with his coattails flapping, he looked like the Wanderer Above the Sea of Fog in Caspar David Friedrich's painting.

When they got back, Alekhine tried to drag him to the bar, but

Neumann was adamant: he would have an apéritif with him if and only if Alekhine would drink nothing more than a glass of seltzer. This prospect made Alekhine desist. Although David was at least ten years younger than him, the violinist was behaving like a big brother. Could he, too, be feeling a nascent sense of friendship?

Neumann left him, agreeing to meet again at dinnertime. Alekhine lingered in the lobby to smoke a cigarette. Meanwhile, other guests had arrived; several suitcases were stacked on a cart being pushed by a porter. Alekhine was again seized by the temptation to head for the bar, but in the end he refrained: sitting there on the high stools were two individuals who were staring at him and whispering to each other. The suspicion occurred to him that they might be agents of the PIDE, Salazar's secret police. He had seen others like them on several occasions: always watchful, keeping to themselves; with their long trench coats and hats, they couldn't have been any more obvious if they'd had labels printed on their foreheads. Sewer rats! They crept around everywhere, at parties, in clubs; they even went so far as to sit at your table in a restaurant, without asking permission. They could arrest anyone on completely arbitrary grounds—a dirty look was enough to land you in jail. Any decent citizen could end up detained for weeks or months, then be released, without the least explanation.

He wondered, with a shudder, what they were doing there; then he turned away and went back to his room.

▪

THE FIRST THING he saw when he opened the door was an envelope that someone had slipped through the crack. It wasn't as bulky as the one he had received earlier; it looked like a simple letter. He was reluctant to open it, but then he braced himself and tore open the flap. Inside, there was only a single photograph, showing him sitting in front of a chessboard playing with Hans Frank. And the kibitzer extraordinaire: Goebbels, minister of propaganda for the Third Reich. It was the photo that had appeared several years earlier on the cover of the magazine *Deutsche Schachzeitung*.

The photograph had been taken in Munich, at the conclusion of a competition in which the German team, headed by himself at the first board, had prevailed. All the players, including him, had been officially invited by several representatives of the Reich to celebrate the victory in a rather sumptuous residence. It was on that occasion that he first met Hans Frank, governor of Poland. An excellent player, obsessed with all things chess, Frank was exhilarated at the thought of being able to speak with the world champion. He invited Alekhine to sit beside him, and all he did was talk about strategy and tactics.

Between this and that, a Berlin Defense or a Dragon Variation, they went on for the entire evening, oblivious to the din and the impromptu choruses that rose around them, distracted only by the need to leap up every now and then, clicking their heels, to raise a glass to the Führer's health. When they left the table, Frank led him to a corner of the room where there were some chessboards. He wanted Alekhine's authoritative opinion on a game he'd recently played.

Just then, without warning, Goebbels appeared, accompanied by a half-dozen officers. Other commitments had kept him from attending the tournament, and he wanted to congratulate the players. His entrance was greeted by prolonged applause. Hans Frank stood to go over to him, but Goebbels gestured for him to remain seated. It was the Reichsminister who came to them. At once, he summoned a photographer to commemorate the moment in the *Deutsche Schachzeitung*. Though he was a player of the lowest level, a simple *Patzer*, being seen with them would make Goebbels look good. So they improvised a game for the benefit of the photographer, who wanted everything to look natural and didn't want anybody posing or looking at the camera. As they began moving the pieces, they inadvertently got involved in a variant of the Vienna Game whose gambit was named after Wilhelm Steinitz, who had devised it. Despite the circumstances, Alekhine couldn't help thinking how ironic it was that, in that den of Nazis, right under the eyes of Reichsminister Goebbels, a Jew should poke his head out, grinning irreverently and making fun of them all. He could just picture Steinitz jumping out of the board, like a kobold with a long reddish beard, similar to those little sprites that pop out of a jack-in-the-box.

Before leaving, Goebbels gave a short speech. He praised the German players, speaking about the importance of chess as a vehicle for the diffusion of the Aryan spirit, before turning to Alekhine and calling him a "friend of the Reich."

■

ATTACHED TO THE photo was another newspaper clipping, which spoke of the Nuremberg trials. The syllogism was glaringly obvious: "Frank and his friends were put on trial, and will most likely be sentenced to death; you were a friend of Frank, and therefore you will meet the same end." A crystal-clear message. There could no longer be any doubt: someone had begun to play a deadly game with Alekhine. And, just as in a game of chess, the attack could come from anywhere, and in the most unexpected way. To his amazement, he discovered that he was no longer afraid: he had faced many death matches in his life, and he would certainly not run from this final threat. Moreover, except for a slight hangover, he felt in excellent shape and even had an appetite. That walk along the shore had definitely done him good.

XIV.

A T A QUARTER to nine, Neumann knocked at the door.

"Come in, David, I'll be ready in just a minute."

Alekhine was still struggling with his tie. He was tempted to tell his new friend about the photo he had received, but then he changed his mind.

"There we are; let's go down," he said, taking him by the arm.

■

THE MOMENT THEY entered the dining room, they were approached by the maître d', who informed them that it would be Senhor Correira's pleasure to have them at his table for dinner. Alekhine could have gladly done without that, but he did not want to appear rude. What's more, glancing around, he realized that there weren't many other free places available. The hotel was gradually filling up, and the strains of a piano drifted from the adjacent dance floor. There were already quite a few people in the room: some who were guests at the hotel, but also others who came there just to have dinner and listen to music.

The maître d' led them to the table, and Correira stood as they arrived, thanking them for the honor shown to him and inviting them to sit down. He went on to make brief introductions: the companion of the woman whom Alekhine, to himself, continued to call the starlet, and who answered to the name of Betty, was Count De Carvajo, and at the head of the table was Dom Enríquez, a high-ranking Spanish prelate. Alekhine could not help noticing that the two men whom he had spotted earlier at the bar were now at a nearby table. Sitting silently by themselves, without their raincoats and hats, in their rumpled jackets and loosened ties, they looked as if they had come to the wrong restaurant. Which was no reason to underestimate them, as he knew all too well. Over the course of his life, it had always been the unassuming people who caused him problems: shabby-looking individuals, indistinguishable from any others, save for the cards they were authorized to pull out of their pockets at any moment.

After Alekhine and Neumann had ordered, the general conversation, interrupted by their arrival, resumed. It was Dom Enríquez who spoke first.

"Evil," he began, not addressing anyone in particular, as if he were giving a sermon, "is an assurance of the gift made to man so that he may do good, which is innate in him. Without the chance to test himself, his earthly journey would have no meaning. If God were to decide to destroy His Adversary, He would deny all creatures the right to free will."

"Ah, there we are, free will!" Correira exclaimed. "Nazi Germany, it seems, managed to produce a new type of individual who gave up the privilege of freedom, of moral choice, and was ready to obey without question, blindly following the dogmas of a political system based on a sort of sanguinary elitism driven to the extreme, and therefore capable of carrying out the most inhuman orders without feeling any remorse. I think that everything that's just taken place has amply shown us that evil can deceive us by disguising itself as good. For that reason, before you even begin to get into the question of free will, I would like to know if we have also been given the capacity to discern between the two. The real danger lies in not recognizing evil once it is already within us. The question, then, is not why God allows evil to exist, but why He permits there to be such a great disparity between the forces of good and the forces of evil." Correira paused briefly. "It would be like a game of chess in which one of the contenders played without the Queen . . . Am I right, Dr. Alekhine?" Without skipping a beat, he continued in a mellifluous tone, looking around at his table companions: "*O doutor Alekhine foi o campeão mundial de xadrez há mais de dezasseis anos.*" Dr. Alekhine has been the world chess champion for over sixteen years.

Count De Carvajo leaned toward the little blonde, who apparently didn't understand Portuguese, and whispered something in her ear; her blue eyes widened, her mouth assuming an expression of ecstatic surprise.

Meanwhile, Correira had resumed the thread of his thought: "It is always a handful of individuals with a mystical aptitude who drive this tremendous force."

"Mystical?" Dom Enríquez asked, bewildered.

"Of course, Monsignor: mystical. Nazism remains incomprehensible to reason precisely because it is of a mystical nature. There is also a mysticism of evil."

"Oh, that's a good one! I don't question the fact that countless wars have been caused and justified by religious fanaticism. But to speak of a mysticism of evil . . ."

"When we talk about the ability to choose between good and evil, we are usually referring to individual behavior," Correira went on, paying no attention to this interruption, "to choices regarding the temptations to which we are all subjected. But these are mere trifles compared with absolute evil. If good is innate in man, we must deduce that evil is a separate entity, which comes from without . . ."

"Comes from without? And from where, if I may ask? From another planet, perhaps?" the clergyman asked sarcastically.

This time, Correira looked directly at him.

"From another divinity. It's the only possible explanation. If there were only one Creator, how could we explain why man has such limited faculties, while evil enjoys unlimited powers?"

"Yours is a Manichaean view," Dom Enríquez retorted sternly.

"Call it whatever you like. However, I wish to point out that Nazi scientists also expressed principles that are completely different from those on which our science is founded. For them, the structure of the universe was based on the two opposing forces of ice and eternal fire. The very fact that we live not on the earth's surface but inside a hollow sphere buried in a mass of ice, and that the celestial vault, as we perceive it, is merely its inner ceiling, should make us reflect."

"Though that did not keep them from almost building the atomic bomb . . ." De Carvajo remarked, before turning his attentions back to the blonde. By now, even the two agents had given up on the theological diatribe and gone back to whispering to each other.

The monsignor, working a seafood fork into the claws of a lobster, tried to bring the discussion back within his realm of expertise. "St. Augustine teaches us that we can only affect those things over which we have control. And God, in His infinite mercy, forgives those who surrender to evil, because He recognizes the power of His Adversary, and knows how difficult it is to resist him."

At those words, to Alekhine's great surprise, the mild-mannered Neumann dropped his knife and fork onto his plate and broke in, clearly upset: "Excuse me, Monsignor, you talk about forgiveness, but don't you think that your God should forgive Himself first of all?"

"What do you mean by that?" the prelate said, bridling. "In what sense should God forgive Himself?"

"I'm referring not only to the war that has led to the destruction of Europe, but, above all, to the systematic extermination of the Jews. Even now, we still have no idea of the immensity of the crime, but you'll see, it won't be long before the facts come to light. In effect, everyone pretended not to know what was happening! And I'm not just talking about some Germanic farmer, who may have been unaware of what was going on behind those walls that rose not far from his pigsties, or the citizen who trusted what he was served up by the press . . . I am referring instead to the complicity of governments, all governments, and the complicity even of your Church!"

Hearing him speak, Alekhine froze. In vastly Catholic Portugal, addressing a high-ranking prelate that way—and, what's more, in the presence of two secret-police agents—could be extremely dangerous. He could not believe that his timid violinist friend had found the courage to open up in that way. Alekhine glanced at the two agents, expecting that at any moment they might flash their cards and drag Neumann away . . . But no one moved. Neumann's words seemed to have turned everyone to stone.

Then, in the pall of silence, Neumann's voice was heard again.

"Among all the lofty concepts articulated this evening, no one has had the courage to broach this subject. Maybe because it doesn't concern pure theological abstractions, but concrete facts, which by now are there for all to see. At Nuremberg, the Nazi leaders confessed to the atrocious truth without batting an eye. And there is irrefutable evidence, besides: photographs of Jews herded into cremation ovens, of skeletons swept away by bulldozers and stacked in piles . . . There is talk of hundreds of thousands of deaths . . ."

"No, no, you're wrong . . ." the monsignor stammered contritely. "No one could have imagined such a thing . . ."

"I must assume," Correira stepped in, "that this tragedy concerns you personally . . ."

Neumann lowered his voice.

"I was the only one of my family to be spared, and only because I was abroad on a tour. Or, rather, my sister survived the camps, but by the time we found each other again, after the war, her health had been completely undermined. She died in November, in Bruges."

"But in the end, you see, good ended up triumphing . . ." the monsignor ventured. At once he realized that his words were completely out of place; he fell silent and took to staring at the lobster remains heaped on his plate.

"And you, Dr. Alekhine, what are your thoughts?"

He'd been expecting this for some time: sooner or later, Correira was bound to target him.

"I think," he said quietly, "that certain tragic events originate from a populace's repressed desires. For hundreds of years, millions of people have gone on believing that Jews are the source of all evil, and that they should be made to disappear from the face of the earth, and suddenly there you have it, the wish comes true. It's a kind of collective prayer, and somewhere or other there is always an evil god around ready to grant it. To go from good to evil is but a short step. We all know that, during a polite conversation at the dinner table, no one could sway us to act immorally. No one could convince us, for instance, that theft is legitimate. But if someone keeps repeating that stealing is, in fact, an act of justice, and that by stealing we are merely redistributing wealth, many will end up believing that man. Especially if he shouts it loudly in the streets, if he holds up symbols and insignia and is acclaimed by the mob. This happened in Russia at the hands of the Bolsheviks, and later in Germany, under the Nazis. The masses always harbor a good dose of resentment toward someone: aristocrats, the bourgeoisie, Jews. Do you really believe that all those people are truly horrified by what happened? Some, maybe, yes, but the majority, though pretending to shudder, inwardly feel a perverse satisfaction. In certain circumstances, human nature is capable of unprecedented acts of baseness—in times of war, insurrection, revolution, when the established order fails, we must always expect that it will be an acquaintance, a relative, a friend who will break down our door in the middle of the night . . . And that's not to mention the silent army we'd see stationed throughout every country in the world if they only had the courage to show their faces: the army of the informers and collaborators."

There: the word had finally come out of his mouth. Pronouncing it, however, he experienced something like a sense of relief. He felt like the criminal who, tired of being hounded by the police, finally decides to turn himself in.

"Indeed, collaborators . . ." Correira murmured, looking him straight in the eye. "Those are the worst of all. Though we can think of the Nazis as automatons, stripped of their souls, and therefore unable to act any differently, informers, on the other hand, must have retained a speck of human conscience. It was their choice, therefore, to side with evil, many driven by personal hatred, by envy, by a desire for profit. Moreover, they were able to operate in the shadows, in anonymity. As a result, they were guilty of inexcusable acts. Yet, despite everything, many will never be punished—they will return to their habitual, respectable lives without being made to pay the price for their sins."

"I don't really think they will get away with it," Count De Carvajo interjected. "Each day, hundreds of bodies are fished out of the Seine. An acquaintance who works at the Foreign Office told me that a list of the names of two hundred thousand collaborators has been

111

compiled in Paris, and that numerous squads of volunteer avengers have already been formed to hunt them down in France and throughout Europe."

"Yet another purge," Alekhine observed. "I can only hope that the list is not in alphabetical order, because if I, too, were on it, given the three 'A's in my name and surname, my head would be one of the first to fall . . ."

It seemed like a good strategy to imply that, though he was not at all unaware of the accusations made against him, he could nevertheless affect the serenity of a man who is sure of his innocence. He tossed the phrase out lightly, as a witty remark. But no one laughed.

■

AT THAT POINT, the strains of Duke Ellington's "It Don't Mean a Thing" started up. In addition to the piano player, a saxophonist and a singer had now appeared in the ballroom. With the war over, military marches had become only a bad memory, and Europe was reviving to the rhythm of swing. The blonde quickly leaped to her feet, grabbed her companion's hand, and urged him to get up. He didn't want to, but after some brief hemming and hawing, he was forced to give in. They set out for the center of the ballroom, lit by a bluish light that now and then verged on violet. Others in the dining room followed their example, and the same fate also ultimately fell to Senhor Correira. Shortly afterward, the prelate and the two plainclothes agents left to go about their business.

When they were alone, Neumann turned to Alekhine.

"Alexandre, there's something I must tell you."

He came around the table and sat down next to him. Before speaking, he looked around guardedly.

"This morning, as I was leaving my room, I surprised someone who was eavesdropping at your door: a burly man, completely bald, with a blunt nose, like a boxer's. When he saw me, he acted like nothing was wrong and walked away. This afternoon, I ran into him again. I was at the reception desk to drop off some letters when he passed by me, headed for the phone booth. He began talking loudly, in an agitated voice. I'd swear he was speaking Russian, or in any case a Slavic language."

"I don't see anything unusual about that."

"The fact is that I heard him say your name a number of times."

Hearing those words, Alekhine felt unsteady, but he quickly composed himself and said, "Being in the same hotel with the world champion, perhaps he wanted to tell a friend."

"A friend? I don't know Russian, but it seems to me that the word *tovarishch* has a different meaning . . ."

"Don't worry, David. Now, however, I'd better turn in. I'm very tired."

■

ONCE IN HIS room, he didn't so much as approach his chessboard, as he usually did, but threw himself on the bed fully clothed without even loosening his tie: he felt exhausted. He closed his eyes, but a noise startled him at once. Someone was fumbling with the lock. He turned quickly to the door and saw the handle lower.

"Who's there?" he called.

No answer. He thought he heard a muffled curse, then footsteps retreating. After that, nothing more. He tried to convince himself that it might be a late-night reveler, distracted or drunk, who had picked the wrong room. Even so, he went rummaging through his bags in search of the double-barreled derringer, a pocket-sized gun he'd carried with him for years; it had once belonged to Nadezhda Fabritskaya. Though it was little more than a cap pistol, and not even loaded, putting it in his pocket gave him a sense of security.

For over an hour, he paced back and forth across the room, pausing every so often to listen at the door. Then, around two o'clock, somewhat calmer, he sat down at the table to write a letter to his wife.

Dear Grace,
You will already have learned the news from the papers. I should feel happy to be back in the limelight, but the truth is that I find myself in a critical situation, because I do not have the money needed to leave the country. I therefore urgently renew my request for a loan from you. The atmosphere in this place is becoming more oppressive each day. I feel as though I have become a persona non grata, as if my presence were an obstacle to the order that is being formed around this new world.
I should get away from here, go directly to England, without setting foot on French soil, where I believe I may be on the blacklist.
I have the sense that the ropes of an invisible net are tightening around me. By now I no longer know where to seek refuge, and at times I think that my only means of escaping death might be death itself . . .

He tore up the letter as soon as he finished it, rewrote it, adding a few variations, then tore it up again. In the end, he decided to give up. There was no point to it except to voice his fears. Seated in the armchair, he fell asleep toward dawn.

XV.

FOR ALEKHINE, THE following days were a period of continual fluctuation between exhilaration and anxiety.

Indeed, starting the following morning, he could see that the Hotel do Parque was filling up like a film set before shooting. The belvedere, the hotel's immense terrace overlooking the ocean, was back in operation, festively decked out with multicolored tents and umbrellas, and in those early-spring days a number of nonguests came to the hotel, too, if only to have lunch and enjoy the warmth of the sun. Part of Alekhine's interview had already appeared in the *Diário de Lisboa*, along with one of the photos of the occasion. Many recognized him and, with one excuse or another, tried to approach him. Just a week ago, he would have given anything to see himself surrounded, once again, by admirers. Now, however, he did his best to avoid them. It wasn't always possible. Though some merely observed him from a distance, others, as if they knew his weakness, invited him to the bar with a pat on the back.

"One more drink, Dr. Alekhine?"

Among the regulars at the brass rail was a certain Mr. Mac-Gregor, from Edinburgh, who, besides a well-equipped golf bag, had brought with him a sample case of whiskey produced by his distillery. In his checkered outfit, complete with knickerbockers and cap, he looked ready to play in a *fin-de-siècle* open on the course at St. Andrews. And then there was Mr. Mulitsch, coffee merchant and art dealer. The latter had appeared before Alekhine with his hand outstretched:

"I'm sure you don't remember me."

"Truthfully, no."

"In '39, you came to our club in Trieste, where you played in a simultaneous match. I was among the participants, and I still cherish the scorecard, which you were good enough to autograph, as though it were a holy relic."

"How many moves?"

"I lasted a good eighteen."

"Ah, yes, I remember: it was a King's Gambit Accepted."

"Extraordinary! What a memory! How do you remember it so precisely?"

"I may forget a face, but never a game."

And then there were also some widows, surely wealthy, all of a certain age, who, unable to take the liberty of a friendly approach, settled for casting him inviting looks from afar. Who knows? he thought. Maybe destiny was offering him one last chance to find a wife, his fifth, ready to pull out her checkbook. For the moment, however, he merely greeted the ladies with a ceremonious bow.

116

Among the new arrivals, he had also noticed a small group of Russians, all male, who kept to themselves; they stood out even from a distance because of the way they were dressed: clothes of mediocre fabric, poorly cut, the jackets always too tight, backs bunched up, and buttons about to pop like champagne corks. Disturbing presences. Who were they? Aimless spies? Or emissaries of the Kremlin sent purposely to observe him? The fact that the Russians totally ignored the presence of the world chess champion made them exceedingly suspicious. No one among them, however, fit the description Neumann had given.

Perhaps, Alekhine thought, he shouldn't call so much attention to himself; yet it was solely around people that he was able to forget his troubles; in public, his darkest shadows paled in the light of reason. At those times, he was certain there must be a logical explanation for all his suspicions, for the fears that assailed him. No, he had to rein in his mind and prevent it from playing nasty tricks on him.

There had been periods in the past when fear of a looming threat had grown to the point of being unendurable. And it was hopeless to try to contain it. On several occasions, he'd had the distinct feeling of being stalked by someone—someone who was just waiting, weapon in hand, for the right moment to attack. In city streets, he took refuge in the crowds, but whenever they thinned out and scattered, and he found himself alone again, it seemed that all the streets led into blind alleys and courtyards with no way out, where the echo of his own footsteps conjured up the approach of an assailant. Perhaps, even more than a knife in the back, he was fearful of being locked up in some monstrous prison, where he would be subjected to unspeakable tortures.

■

HE HAD EXPERIENCED similar anxieties as a child, because of a stupid joke his brother had played on him. One day, Aleksei had brought him to visit the State Historical Museum in Moscow, where Russia's distant past was replicated in tools, utensils, and folk costumes. Along the way, he had lingered in a vast hall where military uniforms and weapons of all kinds were displayed. On a wall, just above a glass case that held knives of various kinds, hung a Tatar saber supported on iron brackets. Seeing that it was within reach, and never imagining that it might be so heavy, Tisha could not resist the temptation to take it down from the wall. In that same moment, however, hearing a guard's footsteps approaching, he'd hurried to put it back in its place—though in his haste he couldn't be sure whether he'd managed to secure it properly. Nevertheless, when the guard arrived, the boy acted as though nothing had happened, and continued wandering through the museum.

Later, when they got home, he confided to his brother that he was worried that the saber might fall on the showcase below it. Aleksei had reassured him, telling him that he would go back to check the following day, and if need be, he himself would see to securing it. But when his brother returned from the museum, his face grim, he brought Tisha tragic news: the saber had come loose from the wall and had fallen, shattering the glass case, and the guard had already given the police a description of the boy who, in his opinion, had caused the damage. Several months passed before Aleksei confessed to him that it had been a joke. Until then, Tisha had lived in terror: the mere sight of a gendarme sent him into a panic, and every time the doorbell rang his heart skipped a beat. He couldn't rid himself of the feeling that the incident was all people were talking about in the city, and he interpreted every look, every word, even the most innocent remark, as an accusation.

■

THERE REMAINED, HOWEVER, the mystery of those photographs slipped under his door. He felt the bastion of rationality that he had painstakingly built waver at the very thought of them. The past came back to weigh on him like a boulder.

One day, Hans Frank had invited him to dine at the officers' table at High Command in Berlin. In a large room, a giant portrait of Hitler flanked by two swastika flags stood out prominently on the bare walls. At the table were half a dozen people, all in uniform. The only one missing was Anton Eher, a publisher in Berlin, who arrived after the others, apologizing for being late. He had the look of a party protégé: pale, bespectacled, hair combed to one side with a part that seemed drawn in chalk, looking as if he had been conceived and born amid stacks of paperwork. He sat down at his place, a bulging leather briefcase resting on his knees, and didn't touch his food, merely accepting a glass of Mosel, with which he barely moistened his lips. At the end of the meal, on Frank's invitation, the guests moved to a private sitting room to smoke and drink cognac undisturbed. Then, as if he had been waiting for just that moment, Eher pulled a small pack of magazines out of the briefcase, newly printed, which he distributed to those present. The caricature of a Jew with an enormous hooked nose and a threatening scowl practically seemed to leap off its chrome-yellow cover. In the upper right corner, a map of Russia was overlaid in red by a hammer and sickle. It was a scientific study, prepared by the Institute for Racial Issues, entitled: *Where Does the Jew's Nose Come From?*

Alekhine, like the others, started leafing through it and, among the uncaptioned photos, recognized a few faces: a Rothschild, Mendelssohn, Chaplin, Werfel, Schnitzler, Einstein . . . Along with the others, a photomontage struck him: a curious double portrait of Emanuel Lasker, a close-up of his face, one crafty eye turned to the lens, while his sleeping Doppelgänger rested his head on his own shoulder.

After skimming through the magazine for some minutes, Frank looked up and said, "Have you ever wondered why the size of the nose gradually gets smaller as you move north?"

No one dared breathe a word: they were all waiting for his answer.

"It's a matter of climate. A prominent nose, in freezing temperatures, would be in danger of snapping in two at the slightest bump." Everyone laughed except Eher, who took the liberty of observing that Negroes also had short, snub noses.

"But their color is enough to distinguish them," Frank exclaimed, triggering more laughter. Finally, he set the magazine down on the coffee table beside him and turned to Alekhine. "It might be more interesting, Dr. Alekhine, if you wrote us an essay on the difference in style between the Aryan game and the Jewish one. We are quite familiar with it—we have often talked about it, remember? It could come out in installments in our newspapers, then ultimately be published as a booklet. The opinion of a world champion would carry some weight. I believe that Dr. Eher here would be happy to publish it; isn't that so?"

"Certainly," the publisher hastened to confirm. "I like the idea."

"By now, we've said everything there is to say about the Jews," Frank went on. "We've talked about their financial swindling, their perverse rituals, the human sacrifices . . . At this point, we certainly wouldn't want to allow them the privilege of distinguishing themselves in chess and considering themselves better than us Aryans. Don't you agree, Dr. Alekhine?"

"Well . . . no, we certainly can't allow that," the master said after a moment's hesitation. "Though I don't think it's easy to demonstrate. It's pure theory."

"A theory that should be reinforced." Frank gave him a hard look. "We'll find a way, you'll see. Meanwhile you write, write."

■

THE PAST: THAT'S what was haunting him. Although he always affirmed with great confidence that everything had been cleared up, he was unable to feel completely reassured. In former times, he had held the job of criminal police investigator, and he knew very well that justice operates nonstop. Persons seemingly above suspicion, who in public behaved quite amicably, changed costumes behind the scenes and assumed other roles: composing dossiers to file in the archives, gathering circumstantial evidence, hearing testimony from witnesses. They prepared the way for the preliminary proceedings, digging into the accused's past, tracing him all the way back to his family. Nothing was overlooked, and any event deemed more or less reprehensible, according to common morality, was taken into consideration. In his case, his mother had died worn out by alcoholism—to be underlined in red. His father had been disowned by the family; that, too, would have to be noted. To top it off, his older brother was said to have taken his own life over a woman—though Alekhine knew perfectly well that it had been an execution ordered by the Kremlin. The fact that he still held the world title was the only element that spoke in his favor.

If only there were someone close to him in whom he could confide . . . But he had lost the company of his friend David as well; the violinist went to Lisbon regularly to rehearse with the orchestra, and sometimes did not even return for dinner.

Toward the end of that week, a visit from his old friend Francisco Lupi took his mind off his obsessive thoughts for a few hours. They spent the afternoon analyzing the possible choices of defense and attack against Botvinnik; toward evening, they took a long walk through the streets of Estoril. Before parting, Alekhine was about to ask him for a loan, but the arrival of a friend of Lupi stopped him.

As he was re-entering the hotel, he realized that he had left his raincoat in the bar where he and Lupi had stopped for a drink. He was tempted to go back, but since in Russia retracing your steps when you are already in sight of your destination is said to bring bad luck, he decided he would return to retrieve it the following day.

XVI.

I T WAS SATURDAY, March 23, the third day of the astronomical spring
of 1946, the first quarter of the waning moon. A gentle breeze from
the southwest wafted off the Atlantic. The daytime temperature had
reached comfortable highs in the shade, and the sky—apart from a
few insignificant cirrus clouds on the horizon—appeared serene and
benevolent. So it seemed at least, though the early return of some
fishing boats suggested otherwise.

That morning, at breakfast time, the terrace overlooking the
ocean was packed. The roar of the waves prevailed over the rustling
of fronds and the screeching of seabirds flapping their wings. On
the colorful striped recliners, men and women raised their faces to the

sun like so many pale heliotropic flowers. The air was so crystalline that even with the naked eye you could see the sailboats setting off from Cascais. Mr. MacGregor scanned the horizon with miniature binoculars. Mr. Mulitsch was negotiating the sale of a gouache by Utrillo with one of the wealthy widows. The two secret-police goons were gone, but Alekhine knew that they would be back. The monsignor had retreated to a quiet corner to read his breviary, and Correira, in the light of that beautiful morning, seemed like the most cordial person in the world.

Sitting in the shade of an awning, with a vermouth at hand and a lit cigarette between his lips, Alekhine was just beginning to feel relaxed when a voice roused him from his thoughts.

"Dr. Alekhine, a promise is a promise."

Correira stood in front of him, with his hale and hearty smiling face.

"Don't you remember the promise you made me a few days ago? A game of chess."

"Forgive me, I had forgotten."

"Come to my table; I have already set up the board."

Alekhine was reluctant to get up, but then he thought that it might be amusing, and, finally, the idea of being able to teach this fellow a lesson revived him completely. He downed his vermouth in one gulp. Despite the promises he'd made to himself, he had decided to delay the start of his detoxification regimen for a few more days. He was therefore in ideal condition to play: not yet having lost his lucidity, but enjoying a slight euphoria.

And yet, approaching a chessboard, even if the challenger was the lowliest of amateurs, never failed to provoke an anxiety not unlike stage fright. Then too, he knew nothing about Correira's abilities. There had been several occasions over Alekhine's career when he had paid the price for underestimating his opponent. Still, he felt obliged to appear generous.

"Senhor Correira, given the disparity of our strengths, you may avail yourself of whichever advantage you deem most appropriate: a Pawn, a Knight, a Rook . . ."

"Thank you, but playing with a handicap would diminish my potential—however unlikely!—victory."

"On the other hand," Alekhine replied, "if I did not grant you an advantage, I would have some difficulty justifying my potential defeat."

"I understand your concern . . . but there might be a way."

"What's that?"

"You could play blindfold. I believe that it's one of your specialties. I'd be curious to see it in operation."

"If that would be enough for you, I agree."

The idea of being able to put on a show excited him. A blindfold game always managed to amaze the public, like certain performances involving hypnosis or mind reading. The layman finds it hard to understand how one can navigate such a complex game without the aid of sight, and many are convinced that there's some trick behind it. He himself, as a child, had been entranced by Pillsbury's skill, and, wanting to imitate him, he had immediately begun practicing with his sister. He soon became aware that he had a gift for it; even at school, during some boring lecture, he could allow himself the luxury of withdrawing in order to play chess without anyone's knowing. Once, during a math quiz, the teacher had asked him abruptly if he had solved the problem. "Certainly. I'll sacrifice my Knight and declare checkmate," he'd replied distractedly, setting the whole class laughing.

Now, after half a century of practice in the game, and thousands of matches stored in his head, playing blindfold against an amateur was the easiest thing in the world: inevitably, in fact, his opponent would fall into a trap right at the opening, and quite likely such a match would end after no more than twenty moves.

After the toss, which assigned him White, Alekhine moved a short distance away, placed a chair next to a table, and sat there, turning his back to the challenger. Then he ordered another vermouth from the waiter.

"I'm ready," Correira said.

Alekhine wanted to show off his skill; to prevent his rival, albeit inexperienced, from locking himself in a Hedgehog Defense and dragging the match on too long, it would be necessary to enter into an open game, if possible with the aid of some gambit, sacrificing one or two Pawns during the very first moves.

As anticipated, after only a few strokes, Correira, lured by this easy material gain, made his first error, which weakened his castling. Nevertheless, his position was not completely compromised yet: there remained a single line of defense, which Correira was careful not to follow, convinced that he had the advantage. Alekhine remembered having played a game very similar to this twenty years ago, in Baden-Baden, against a student, and many other grandmasters of the past had successfully tried it. All in all, there was no imagination required; he didn't even have to make an effort to visualize the position of the pieces in his mind, because he knew the moves from memory. So, while his opponent was sweeping up Knights and Bishops purposely left unprotected, Alekhine was tightening the noose. And, in fact, before they reached the twentieth move, he announced checkmate. Behind him there was a round of applause. A knot of curious onlookers had already gathered around the board. Correira seemed to have taken the blow badly. Perhaps he'd expected to hold out longer, or even be able to draw. Alekhine approached the board and, having reconstructed the position, quickly showed him the places where his greed had led him to make mistakes.

Correira immediately demanded a rematch, which he was granted. This time he would play White.

Alekhine returned to his seat.

Correira opened with the Queen's Pawn: an opening that for a good player holds no big surprises from Black. At least in the initial moves, Correira did not make any mistakes and came out of the opening positioning his pieces correctly. That he had come that far, however, was clearly due to the fact that he had slavishly memorized the initial moves of a very popular game. The so-called Queen's Gambit does not lend itself to spectacular maneuvers, but it does involve internal strategies that are completely obscure to the layman. Correira certainly did not strike Alekhine as a great strategist, and soon appeared to be completely mired.

Meanwhile, the crowd of onlookers behind Alekhine must have swelled. Alekhine could hear them clearly as they offered advice, and someone must have gone even further, because Correira loudly ordered the offender to take his hands off the chessboard. Then, abruptly, the excited whispering ceased altogether, and for a few minutes a troubling silence ensued. Finally, with unusual confidence, his opponent announced his move:

"Knight takes Bishop!"

"Rook takes Knight," Alekhine shot back.

But at that point something inexplicable happened: an unforeseen move, a Pawn Push that Alekhine had not taken into account, completely overturned the fate of the game.

Too decisive, too immediate a response for one who until that moment gave every indication of floundering in quicksand. Whereas only a minute before he'd been ready to launch a counterattack, Alekhine now had to fall back. He'd been under the illusion that the game would unfold as before, without consequences or risks, but instead his opponent was gaining the upper hand. Was it possible that Correira was a far stronger player than he let on, and that he had lost the first game on purpose, to be able to make up for it with the second? From that point on, Alekhine was subject to a relentless attack. He had to resort to all of his mastery to prevent the promotion of a Passed Pawn, and in the end barely managed to reach the safe haven of a draw by Perpetual Check. The match had lasted far longer than he'd expected, and for many of the spectators, those who loved to see fireworks, had turned out to be disappointing.

His vision blurred by a reddish haze, Alekhine went over to congratulate his opponent through clenched teeth, as the latter flashed a triumphant smile. Seeing him gloat, Alekhine realized that Correira was gradually claiming all credit for that success. He supposed it was human nature for a dying man, once cured, to characterize a genuinely miraculous escape as being due to his own natural fortitude. Behind him, however, was the prompter, still intent on moving the pieces on the board, analyzing the countless variations of the match just played. Only a master was capable of doing it so assuredly. Curious, they all watched this man who had appeared out of nowhere and was now flaunting his skills. He was burly, bald, with a pushed-in face and a blunt nose, typical of a boxer, just like the individual described to Alekhine by Neumann. Alekhine didn't think he had ever seen him before.

"My congratulations, Senhor Correira," Alekhine said, extending his hand, "though I am inclined to think that this was not all your own doing."

At those words, the prompter looked up from the board, gave a slight bow, and, addressing him in Russian, said, "Gospodin Alekhine, forgive my intervening, but the temptation was too strong."

"I realized it right away. There are no such things as miracles, much less on the chessboard. I don't believe I know you, however, Mr. . . ."

"Boris Boronov."

The name, very common in Russia, meant nothing to Alekhine.

"We met several years ago."

"Really? I don't recall."

"Perhaps it will refresh your memory if I tell you that one should not invite a lady to waltz if one has had one too many shots of *rakia* . . ."

BLED, SLOVENIA, 1931. Undefeated winner of the tournament, Alekhine had celebrated by getting drunk, and no sooner had the orchestra struck up the notes of a Strauss waltz than he got to his feet, legs unsteady, and dragged a slender lady, the wife of one of the participants, to the middle of the dance floor with him. After leading her through a couple of dizzying pirouettes, he tripped, and they both ended up stretched out on the shiny parquet.

At that time, he was still married to Nadezhda Fabritskaya, his third wife, though their marriage had already come to an end: the "saintly woman," as he called her, was not only loath to accompany him on his tours, but had by then been pushed beyond the limits of her endurance, and, breaching all etiquette, could no longer keep from heaping abuse on Alekhine in public, employing epithets not at all in keeping with her noble upbringing, the kindest of which was "*russkaya svin 'ya*"—that is, "Russian swine."

"IT WAS A regrettable incident," Alekhine said, "though fortunately without serious consequences for the poor lady. I don't, however, recall any Boronovs who participated in that tournament."

"I was there as a mere spectator. It was I who helped you up, before the lady could suffocate beneath you, Dr. Alekhine."

"At this point, all I can do is thank you."

Then, to avoid any further overtures, Alekhine turned abruptly and walked away, without another word.

XVII.

H E WENT DOWN the staircase leading to the beach and set out toward the lighthouse. He was in a foul mood, furious with himself; he still couldn't forgive himself for having let that Boronov steal the scene from him. Who was he? And what was he doing there? Could he be from the NKGB? Alekhine was again assailed by qualms and uncertainties. He recalled the words of Miss Ocampo, who, during the interview, had asked him if he wasn't afraid of being assassinated. Only now that he thought about it was he beginning to realize that he was involved in a challenge with uneven odds. The two envelopes of newspaper clippings and photographs slipped under his door were a clear warning.

Who was it he had to watch out for? Correira? The prelate? Count De Carvajo? Or one of the new arrivals—that Mulitsch, for example, or MacGregor? And now this Boronov had also appeared, a chess master by sheer coincidence, who addressed him as *gospodin*, "esteemed master," not without a note of sarcasm. And if Neumann claimed to have heard him say the word *tovarishch*, "comrade," then he was certainly not an émigré.

■

ALEKHINE WENT ON walking, and was deep in thought when he heard shouts; looking up, he saw some young men not far from him, standing in water up to their waists, struggling to drag ashore what looked like remains. As he drew nearer, he made out a shapeless mass, maybe a conger eel, or a sea lion, with its alveoli in shreds. Jostled by the waves, it spun around, exposing a soft underbelly covered with dozens of swollen teats. Impossible to determine what it was. It looked like a giant cirrhotic liver. He had never seen anything so repulsive. The boys kept jabbing long stakes into the amorphous body, but only a purulent fluid oozed out of the wounds, and the creature, though it was now largely decomposed, gave the impression of moving its eyes, as though it were still alive and suffering from the blows inflicted on it. An aborted line of evolution, unclassifiable in any atlas of natural history, yet resembling—Alekhine wasn't sure why—a human being.

"Leave it alone!" he shouted, but his voice was lost in the roar of the surf.

He hurried away, averting his eyes from the macabre spectacle, and started walking again, as all his doubts and anxieties came flooding back to fill his head. Was he still capable of holding his own in a match for the world title? The stalemate a short time ago had deeply troubled him. The stranger, that Boronov, had not only made him look ridiculous, but also undermined Alekhine's confidence in himself. That

Pawn Push could only have been the result of scrupulous theoretical analysis. Being forced to a draw by a chess player whom he had never heard of compelled him to reconsider his assessment of the Soviet school: if an anonymous master was capable of that, who knew what heights the preparation of their incumbent champion had reached? He pictured his young challenger, utterly committed to his training, and for that reason attended not only by assistants ready to analyze hundreds of variations for him, but also by a team of doctors who, in addition to prescribing a strict diet, divided his day into hours for study and time for physical activities. And while this enormous crew was readying a war machine to destroy him, here he was, alone, in this place on the coast, his spirit stricken, his body falling apart, exactly like the marine monster he had just seen. If he were to lose the match with Botvinnik, he would no longer have a future, or anywhere to go. Better to die, Alekhine thought, rather than suffer defeat.

Just then, an acute pain stabbed through his chest. It wasn't the usual dull, diffuse ache, but as if a crack had opened in the frozen surface of a lake. He had forgotten that, among his many opponents, real and imagined, there was another, far more formidable. Though he kept walking, breathing in shallow gasps, he felt his strength abandon him. Doubled over by the agonizing pain, he made his way to an old wrecked boat stranded onshore and, sagging onto the sand like a hot-air balloon, leaned against the keel for support. His distress was becoming more severe. It was as if someone had stuck a marlinspike in his sternum and were turning it to widen the wound. Only after several minutes did the stabbing pain diminish before disappearing altogether. He remained where he was, unmoving, for fear that the pain might resume. In the blinding light, flocks of petrels, plunging from great heights, dove into the water, to re-emerge and be rocked by the waves, like ducks in a carnival shooting gallery. Perhaps it was true that by observing their flight one could predict the approach of a storm. Didn't the ancient augurs predict a man's fate that same way?

Outlined against the horizon he saw the silhouette of a ship coming from Gibraltar and headed for the port of Lisbon. If only he had enough money to leave this place, his wife, Grace, would surely put him up until the date of the match. But France was too dangerous for him. Besides, where would he get the money? He was again tempted to ask Lupi for a loan. Or Neumann. Wasn't the business of money lending characteristic of the Jews? If he sold his Hamilton wristwatch and gold tiepin, he wouldn't get much. There was only one possibility of raising the money needed to pay for the trip, but just the thought of having to part with his Sèvres vase made him shudder. Perhaps he could take it to a pawnshop, then redeem it later on, once the match with Botvinnik was over. But how can one part with one's talisman at the most critical moment of one's lifetime?

He closed his eyes. The sun warmed his lowered eyelids; the screeching of the petrels grew fainter, more distant. He dozed off for a few minutes, or so it seemed.

■

HE FOUND HIMSELF walking down a country lane, along with his mother and his brother and sister, retracing the route they used to take in early spring. The birches all wore a collar of pale-pink crocuses at the base of their trunks, and the meadows, still yellowed, were dotted with persistent patches of grayish snow and thin crusts of ice, beneath which flowed rivulets of water—simply touching them with your toe made them splinter, crunching like caramelized sugar. The family was headed toward the alder woods, and from there they would go down to the Moskva River. Aleksei led the way, with the air of a platoon captain; picking up a dry branch that the snow's weight had snapped off and brandishing it like a weapon, he enjoyed stabbing the air, attacking an invisible enemy. Then, abruptly, Aleksei vanished on the horizon, and Varvara and his mother dissolved as well, leaving only the luminous trace of their strikingly similar smiles. All of a sudden, Alekhine was an adult again, in the midst of a crowd gathered in front of a stage on which a children's play was being performed. The young actors were wearing white tunics, and their foreheads were encircled by laurel wreaths. Alekhine himself, soon afterward, would have to get up on that stage and give a speech, yet he could not remember a single word of it; he knew, however, that he had written it all down, and kept looking through his pockets for his notes, which somehow slipped through his fingers and ended up trampled in the crush. So he turned to a man standing beside him and asked him what it was about, and though the man repeated it to him several times, he could not hear what he was saying. As Alekhine made his way through the crowd, heading for what now seemed like a gallows, people expressed their pity for him: "He's not up to it. He's no longer what he once was. He'll never manage it." At the height of despair, he invoked the Almighty, begging Him to spare His servant this humiliation and ridicule. But when the time came to climb onto the stage, Alekhine saw that there was a prelate with a long beard up there waiting for him. The latter, pointing his finger at him, shouted: "Prepare, good Christian, because for you the Day of Judgment is approaching, as unexpected as thunder in spring."

■

AT THAT HE woke up. The waves, now higher, crashed against a rocky outcropping. A bit of spray reached Alekhine's sun-reddened face. Suddenly, the form of a man loomed in front of him, obscuring the sun; backlit, his face was dark. The indistinct figure, appearing out of the blue, struck Alekhine as ominous, and when the man bent over him, he feared for his life and raised his hands to his chest, palms out, in a defensive gesture. Only then did he hear the sound of a familiar, reassuring voice.

"Alexandre, what's happened to you?"

"It's you, David, thank God."

Neumann reached down and helped him up.

"Did you feel ill?"

"I have a bad heart, David."

Alekhine was confused and embarrassed. He looked into his friend's face and thought he saw a look of reproach and pity. That was enough. He didn't need to add anything more. Alekhine knew all too well that he needed to put an end to his intemperances.

They returned to the hotel in silence. He was relieved to see that the boys were gone, and that the ocean had sucked the marine monster back into its belly. Alekhine leaned on his friend's shoulder. He who abhorred any physical contact, even a handshake, at that moment of utter depletion took a vague comfort in it. As they climbed back up the stairs, he stopped several times to catch his breath.

As soon as they reached the lobby, the chef came to meet them. It was the first time he'd made an appearance. He was short, plump enough to represent his profession credibly, and wore a starched white toque on his head.

"Dr. Alekhine," he exclaimed, waving his hands about excitedly, "tonight there will be a dinner in your honor. Such exquisite delights, you'll see! And such wines!"

Recalling the putrid remains of the marine monster, Alekhine could not suppress a look of revulsion, and the chef, who had not missed it, hastened to add: "Of course, I am aware of your tastes. You'll sample cuts of select prime meats, savor my filet of beef Stroganoff, and then the desserts: *crema catalana*, and even a rich torte."

"Don't say another word," Alekhine cut in, "don't ruin the whole surprise for me." In fact, one more word would have been enough to turn his stomach.

Neumann accompanied him up to his room. He insisted on

staying with his friend long enough to make sure Alekhine was completely recovered.

"So they've decided to throw me a party," Alekhine said. Then, in silence, he took the envelopes with the newspaper clippings from the shelf and emptied their contents on the table.

"Someone slipped these under my door."

Neumann glanced at the articles. Finally, his attention lingered on the cover of the *Deutsche Schachzeitung* portraying Alekhine with Goebbels and Frank. The photo must have made a deep impression on him: he couldn't take his eyes off it.

"So it's all true, what they say about you," he murmured.

Alekhine lowered his head in a gesture of infinite despair. Neumann seemed to have turned to stone. Something remote, like the mark of an ancient, noble lineage, showed in his features. That expression, hurt and stunned at the same time, reminded Alekhine of the face of an old man he had seen in Warsaw five years before, a sight that left an indelible impression in his mind. He had run across the man along a bridge over the Vistula, being forcibly dragged off by two young men in uniform, little more than adolescents: a small Jew with a long gray beard, the collar of his jacket tattered, his glasses, with their thick, convex lenses, hanging crookedly on his face. As the old man tried to free an arm to straighten them, the younger of the two boys, with a punch to the back of his neck, sent his hat and glasses flying into the murky waters below. Seeing a boy strike a defenseless old man—an act so abominable, so contrary to human nature— Alekhine had wanted to intervene, but at the last moment his courage failed him and he stepped aside, raising his outstretched arm in a salute. It was a memory of which he was not proud; it epitomized the extreme weakness of his character.

"Believe me, David, I had to do it: my wife's life was at stake, and mine as well. As for me, I did nothing wrong, all I did was play chess."

"For their glory . . ." Neumann said, a profound bitterness in his voice.

"Those games are still *my* games, even though I was forced to play under their flag."

Neumann put the photograph back on the table and walked to the window, where he looked out into the distance.

"What are you thinking, David?"

Neumann hesitated. Then he began speaking in a low voice, barely audible.

"I was on tour in America when I learned of the deportations in Belgium. At the time, I had to direct an orchestral piece for wind and string instruments. It was one of my own compositions, inspired by Schumann's *Davidsbündler*, music that I have lost all interest in performing since then. While I was directing David's march against the Philistines, the Hitlerjugend was marching on Europe. At night, though I woke up gripped by anxiety, it was not the fate of my family that concerned me, but that of my work, which was about to be performed for the first time. It didn't occur to me that at that moment those dear to me might already have been arrested. Instead, my concern was that the entry of the flute be perfectly executed, and that the bassoon's response be in sync with the oboe . . ."

He turned back to Alekhine, pale, his face suffused with grief.

"I believe that art has the power to make us forget everything, to turn us away from affections, from obligations, to make us exceedingly egoistic, obliterating any trace of love in us." He rubbed his forehead. "I wonder," Neumann continued, "if talent is a gift or a curse. I wonder why we have not been granted the prospect of reconciling art with life, why the two paths diverge to such an extent. But it is art and not life that fulfills our deepest desires. And we succumb to its lure. That is why, at times, I fear that there will be no redemption for us." He waved a hand as if to chase away a troubling thought. "I think you should leave this place, Alexandre. There is a ship about to set sail from Lisbon for England."

"I can't leave yet," Alekhine said. "I'm waiting for the official telegram from London." He wanted to add that he didn't have the money to pay for a ticket, but he couldn't bring himself to do it.

"I'm sorry not to be able to attend your party. Tonight I'm busy with rehearsals for tomorrow's concert. But I have already reserved an orchestra seat for you at the Teatro Nacional."

"I will do everything I can to be there, I promise."

"Now I really must go," Neumann said. "They've already come to take my bags—they're waiting down below. After the concert, I will embark on that ship."

"You mean we won't see each other again?"

"I'm counting on seeing you tomorrow night, sitting in the front row."

Alekhine walked him to the door. In the doorway, they both hesitated for a moment, then embraced awkwardly, like two people unaccustomed to such effusions.

"I will miss the music of your violin."

"Take care of yourself, Alexandre," Neumann said. It sounded like a farewell.

As soon as he closed the door, Alekhine felt the full weight of loneliness fall upon him. He returned to his armchair, to his chessboard. It felt as if a century had passed since the last time he had performed that ritual. The chess pieces seemed distant to him. Divested of their function, they were merely a jumble of useless figurines in carved wood. He could hardly bear to look at them. What strange evil spell had been cast over him? To counter this unusual apathy, he had to resort to his talisman: the Sèvres vase that had accompanied him throughout his life. He stood up, took it very carefully from its case, and for a long time held it in his hands—but he realized, to his dismay, that he felt no benefit from this contact. He still remembered the time when he had found it damaged, and how he had carefully saved the tiny fragment of porcelain, no bigger than the nail of his little finger, finally to entrust it to the hands of the finest ceramicist. Now not even the eye of an expert would notice the restoration. He walked over to the window to look at the vase in full light. For him, it represented the only real possibility of salvation.

But the moment always comes, he thought, when all our illusions fail, and with them every amulet that might protect us, that might still prove auspicious: talismans, formulas, prayers, sacred images . . . all of them. Death must be faced by ridding yourself of all this panoply: going without weapons, without shields or armor. Approaching death as naked as you were at birth.

After contemplating his Sèvres vase for the last time, Alekhine threw it firmly out the window.

XVIII.

I T IS NINE o'clock in the evening when Alekhine leaves his room. The dinner in his honor will be held in a private room, with a small number of guests, well apart from the noisy dance floor. The space has been decorated for the occasion: There are even festoons of colored paper suspended from the central chandelier. Flickering candelabras illuminate the table, laden with elegant blue porcelain plates and solid silver cutlery. A battery of crystal glasses of every shape and size heralds a satisfying tasting of fine wines.

His entry is greeted by applause. Seated at the table, in addition to the Correiras, Dom Enríquez, and Count De Carvajo, are several new faces, and some old acquaintances as well: Carlos Peres, Castaldo

Branco, Virgilio Suares, Portuguese chess players he met several years before in Lisbon. Only Betty, the starlet, is missing, apparently stricken by a migraine. The unexpected welcome flatters him and fills him with pride. Senhor Correira makes a first toast, singing the praises of Alekhine's eminence as a chess player. In the glow of the candelabras, the guests' eyes light up with a strange gleam, as if in expectation of something more. In due time, Alekhine notices that Miss Ocampo is also among the guests, barely recognizable in an evening dress and elaborate hairdo.

The bombastic panegyric ends, and he realizes that they're expecting a response from him. Alekhine abhors public speaking, and the only topic that he enjoys addressing is chess; he therefore responds briefly, thanking Correira for his words and urging everyone not to keep the waiters, who are ready to serve, waiting any longer.

■

THE TROLLEYS WITH the dishes are brought in: compliments must be paid to the chef's inventiveness. These are truly artistic creations, fanciful structures composed of tangles of tentacles, slimy mollusks, and fish in a rainbow of colors. For Alekhine, however—as for a spoiled, picky child—only small morsels of steak tartare and carpaccio, accompanied by a fine selection of red wines—Aragonês, Touriga, Baga—flavorful, as strong as liqueurs. Behind him, a waiter stands ready to fill his glass as needed.

The sumptuous appetizer is savored in an almost ritual silence; then, as the waiters remove the dishes, someone from the end of the table asks him: "Dr. Alekhine, how many games have you played in your life?"

"I estimate having played more than fifty thousand."

"Do you believe that to play chess well one must have a penchant for mathematics?"

"I don't think a knowledge of mathematics is useful. Personally, I'm not at all inclined toward numbers."

"And yet it is always a matter of exercising a capacity for calculation. How many moves do you have to be able to predict in advance?"

"Sometimes, in response to one of our moves, the opponent may be faced with a number of different possibilities, and we can, in turn, respond to each of these likely moves with a number of further moves . . . In which case, the combinations are too numerous and would require an infinite amount of time to be able to analyze one by one. So we must rely on our general sense of the position, and on instinct. When, however, instead of multiple options, the possibilities are reduced, then calculation becomes easier."

"And how important is memory?"

"I remember thousands of games, from the first move to the last."

Questions start pouring in from all sides. But he doesn't feel at all uncomfortable: indeed, he's found himself in similar situations many times, and even enjoys it.

Miss Ocampo, sitting not far from him on the other side of the table, also chimes in. "Dr. Alekhine, during our recent meeting I neglected to ask you if you've played with many women over the course of your career."

"I have played with a number of women, including, of course, my last wife."

"And do you think women have a proclivity for the game of chess?"

"I wouldn't say so. I can say that my mother was a good player, but, generally speaking, no, they do not, and during my career I have known only one woman capable of competing at the highest levels: Vera Menchik."

"How do you explain that? Maybe because chess is a simulation of war, and therefore of primarily masculine interest? Or is it perhaps a question of intelligence?"

"Of intelligence? Oh, not really. I think it is simply a matter of *forma mentis.*"

"Very interesting," Correira joins in. "A biological view of chess, which could be extended to a broader field: the anthropological sphere. One may wonder why chess is more prevalent in the North than in the South, and why it arouses so much interest among certain peoples, and among others is completely ignored."

"The cradle of chess was Russia," Alekhine says without hesitation.

"There are some who say," Correira goes on in an insinuating tone, "that the best chess players are Russian Jews. In second place would be non-Jewish Russians, then non-Russian Jews, and lastly everyone else, neither Russians nor Jews."

"I could give you a long list of non-Jewish Russians who were true masters of our time."

"Nevertheless, it's thanks to the Jews who were persecuted and driven out of Russia, or forced into exile, that chess later became widespread in Central Europe and over the rest of the world. And over the course of your career, you've had occasion to encounter many Jews."

"A great many."

"In your opinion, do Jews therefore have a predisposition for chess?"

"That's a thorny question," Alekhine replies, unfazed. "After more than thirty years of experience, I can say that, yes, Jews have the practical skill to exploit the game, but up till now there hasn't been a single Jew who has shown any artistic qualities."

"Not even one?" Correira presses him.

Alekhine conceals a surge of impatience by asking the waiter to pour him some more wine, and then, looking directly at his questioner, says, "Lasker, perhaps, with his concept of 'struggle.' As a boy, I had boundless admiration for him. His comments on the games played at the St. Petersburg tournament in 1908 are a clear example of the profundity of his thinking. The tournament book was truly invaluable to me. Then, too, unlike some others, he had the decency not to come up with any outlandish theories, the way certain people did . . ."

"Dr. Alekhine," Correira interrupts with cold determination in his voice, "several of your articles appeared in Nazi newspapers, in particular the *Pariser Zeitung*, in a series entitled 'Aryan and Jewish Chess,' whose subtitle implies that Jews lack courage and creativity."

So, Alekhine thinks, here we go: the past is coming back.

"In those articles," Correira continues, his tone increasingly sharp, "you claimed to demonstrate the superiority of the Aryan race over the Jews, and behind your words was an indisputable apologia for Nazism: no Jew is spared by you, not even Lasker. It is difficult to see how your supposedly genuine adoration for him could so suddenly have changed into an attitude of superiority, if not contempt. At one time you wrote: 'Lasker was my teacher, the concept of chess as art would have been unthinkable without him.' Then, overnight, you changed your mind. In the articles in question, you in fact maintained that with Lasker's defeat the chess world was finally rid of the Jewish specter, and that this was to Capablanca's credit.

"Now that the war is over, those same ideas have precluded the possibility of your participating in major international tournaments. A number of chess players—not all of them Jewish—have even threatened to withdraw should you enter a competition. And yet you admit that you wrote those articles yourself, isn't that so? In your own words?"

"This is not the first time I've had to answer that question," Alekhine replies, his voice firm. "I did not write them myself. Or, rather, I wrote them only in part. Later, without my knowledge, phrases and thoughts were inserted that were not mine, transforming a purely theoretical opinion into a highly defamatory statement, and completely distorting my thinking. I should point out that there was nothing offensive about the Jewish people in those original pages, and that my criticisms were instead directed against certain ideas spread by a small group of Jewish theoreticians who debased the art of chess, reducing it to mere theoretical exercise."

"But at the root of it all there was, therefore, a personal conviction," Correira concludes, with a false, conciliatory smile.

Alekhine does not appear to have felt the blow. Lowering his voice, he resumes speaking calmly. "I will try to clarify the concept. I can only do so by resorting to comparisons. Take, for example, painting: there are many young people, just out of the academy, capable of turning out highly accurate drawings, which nonetheless appear lackluster, lifeless, mere illustrations typical of a glossy magazine. Whereas others, with a few brushstrokes, are able to render the essence, the very soul of the subject."

"Forgive me," Correira says in a faintly ironic tone, "but I fail to see the connection between painting and chess. Explain it better."

Alekhine doesn't bat an eye: he is resolutely determined to answer any question, to dodge any trap set by his inquisitor. He does so with the patient air of a schoolmaster who wants to explain a simple concept to a dense student.

"Chess is not—as many believe—a simple board game. It rises to the status of art—not only for the sheer number of possible combinations, but above all for the unique concept of 'checkmate.' Therein lies the allure and beauty of chess, which even the layman unconsciously perceives. It represents an ideal that must be attained through joyful self-sacrifice."

Suddenly he realizes that neither Correira nor the other guests will, perhaps, be able to understand a word of this desperate peroration, but by then he can't stop himself, and he surges on impetuously: "That's why the notion of art shines through this magnificent game, and why the innermost spirit that inspires it corresponds perfectly to creative vision, which demands total self-abnegation. The comparison to painting thus serves to clarify the connection between technique and art."

"Indeed, you have always viewed chess from an artistic standpoint," his disputant observes wryly. "It's up to you, therefore, to enlighten us on this age-old problem: tell us, where does technique end and art begin?"

"Art is impossible to define. It can, however, be recognized, and one of the indicators of art is risk. Without risk there can be no creation. And I look to this to explain the Jewish conception of chess. It can be traced to two fundamental tenets: first, material gain at all costs; second, opportunism driven to the extreme, which, determined to avoid every conceivable risk, goes so far as to formulate the idea—if it can be called that—of defense at any cost. In other words, the elimination of risk. It is quite true that if a player maintains his defense he will manage to avoid defeat. But one is instinctively led to ask: how can he ever win? Perhaps the answer might be: by waiting for the opponent to make a mistake. But if this mistake never happens? Then all the defender *à tout prix* can do is complain about the lack of mistakes. But you don't get rich by saving! You don't get anywhere by standing still. With its principle of avoiding any form of danger, Jewish chess denied itself any possibility of growth. And even that isn't the problem, as such—everyone should play as he sees fit—but, rather, the fact that an 'inadequacy' can be passed off as absolute truth. All of this began in fact with Nimzowitsch and his book *My System*, and continued with Réti and his treatise *Modern Ideas in Chess*, a work that was greeted with jubilation by Anglo-Jewish pseudo-intellectuals. This shameful deception spread rapidly and, like an epidemic, infected the entire chess world. Even Capablanca was influenced by it. Attending Columbia University in New York, the Jewish capital, this acclaimed child prodigy—the idol of the Latin world, who could have become a worthy heir to Morphy—ended up giving in to temptation. Capablanca had already seen in chess the opportunity for material gain, and then, suppressing his remarkable innate qualities, pushed the Jewish principle of 'safety above all' to the limit."

Alekhine pauses to take a breath: he's getting too worked up, he knows, and fears his heart will suffer for it.

"To some it may seem strange that I would go on so much about a simple difference of opinion in the chess world," he continues in a calmer tone. "None of this would have affected me very much had those views remained mere theories. My perspective on the matter changed when I found that those theories had become a concrete threat directed against me. Because a theory must also be demonstrated in practice, and in this case on the chessboard. If I were defeated by a supporter of this doctrine, the notion would be reinforced, and might continue its rampage unopposed. The Jewish collective had already spelled out its principles in '35, in my match against Max Euwe: they were published throughout the world, thanks to specialized magazines that always included several Jewish contributors. But never could I have imagined that Dr. Euwe—that peaceable, sportsmanlike, cultured, affable individual—would consent to being used as their guinea pig! There was obviously a conspiracy against me: the match was organized by a group composed entirely of Jews, and I was forced to take as my second the Dutch master Samuel Landau, also a Jew, who at the decisive moment of the competition left me in the lurch for 'personal reasons.' Only then did I realize that it was not Euwe I was playing against but, rather, an entire team. I lost the title by half a point, but in the rematch I triumphed in a ten-to-four win: it was a humiliating defeat for the Jewish cabal."

"Max Euwe, as I understand it, is not Jewish," Correira points out.

"No, but he completely embraced their theories and allowed himself to be manipulated by the Jews for their own purposes."

"When you talk about their theories, are you referring to all Jewish players or just some?"

"It only takes one bad master to create a legion of followers."

"Dr. Alekhine"—Correira's tone is increasingly ironic, almost mocking—"only a moment ago, you repudiated the content of those

146

articles, asserting that they had been deliberately altered. Now, however, it seems that all you're doing is quoting yourself. Your words reveal a strong racial aversion toward the entire Jewish people."

I should not have offered explanations to this rabble, Alekhine thinks. But by now he's gone too far, and perhaps has already passed the point of no return. He knew he was on trial and that he had to prepare a strong defense. Although he'd promised himself he'd be cautious in his statements, just now he feels he must go on the offensive. Even in chess, moreover, he has often very carefully prepared a variation to play, only to reject it at the last moment in favor of a diametrically opposite strategy. By this time, he's had enough of the prudent good sense that he has feigned so far. The wine has put him in an argumentative mood. They expect him to confess to his sins? Okay, then, here they are! He even feels a perverse satisfaction in making matters worse, like a self-confessed murderer who assumes a confrontational attitude in court, not only blatantly refusing to show repentance, but going so far as to describe the most gruesome details of his crime.

"I wish to stress that I have nothing against their race, I have nothing against Jewish doctors, scientists, or musicians. I am only speaking of those whom I encountered in the world of chess. My outrage is simply due to the way some of them have debased my beloved game. And don't talk to me about intolerance, prejudice, or racism. The aversion—not to say hatred—toward goyim, outsiders, originates, if anywhere, with the Jews themselves! They are the first to consider themselves the chosen race. Rubinstein felt it in his blood, having learned it as a boy at Hebrew school. I'll give you just one example: After a tournament held in Triberg—in which I participated as an arbiter, not as a player—I asked Rubinstein why he had decided on a certain move in the opening, a move that was unquestionably inferior to the one I had played against Bogolyubov a few months before, which, after a thorough analysis, was found to be unassailable. Yes, it's a good move, he said, but it is still a *foreign* move. Not to mention the Jew from Riga, Aron Nimzowitsch, who openly hated us Slavs. At the end of the tournament in New York, in 1927, I had an exchange of words with him that I am unlikely to ever forget. Nimzowitsch had been outclassed by me and then defeated in more than one match by the Slovenian grandmaster Milan Vidmar. So, one evening, out of spite, he brought the conversation around to the Soviets and came out with a phrase that was clearly meant to offend us: 'Anyone who says "Slav" is saying *slave*.' To which I replied: 'But anyone who says "Jew" has actually already said it all.'

"After the defeat of Emanuel Lasker, Rubinstein and Nimzowitsch proclaimed themselves Capablanca's official challengers. Rubinstein was the first to throw down the gauntlet at the world champion, who immediately declared himself ready. Following my successes of that time, however, all the experts recognized that Rubinstein was no longer up to calling himself Capablanca's challenger. In fact, the following year, he wasn't even invited to New York for the international tournament. And this allowed the Rubinstein matter to be permanently closed. Shortly thereafter, however, another threat cropped up in the form of the same Aron Nimzowitsch. When I say 'threat,' I should point out that although the Jew from Riga did not stand the slightest chance of beating Capablanca, even his 'honorable defeat' could be used in favor of the aforesaid theories. He, too, therefore, had to be eliminated from the competition. Beating him first in Semmering, in 1926, and then in New York and Kecskemét, in 1927, I forced him to step aside and clear the way for me."

"Nevertheless," Count De Carvajo remarked insinuatingly, "Nimzowitsch is assured of an important place in the history of chess, partly due to the defense that bears his name, isn't that so?"

"Simple opportunism! The merit of any discovery is generally accorded not so much to its legitimate inventor as to the one who takes the first opportunity to pass it off as his own. An opening is employed countless times, and then someone comes along and says, 'Hey, I like this defense. I'll put my name on it before someone else does.' But if every master were to give his name to a variant . . . Anderssen won a match against Morphy opening with the Rook's Pawn in a3, but he certainly didn't think of giving his name to an opening that not even a child would have played. I, on the other hand, can say that I did in fact devise a defense, wholly my own, which had never been played before, and so there is good reason for it to bear my name—even if it is not used much, being too complex to fall within every player's grasp. Nimzowitsch was a master of self-promotion, and because of that he has enjoyed an undeserved renown. Beyond which, I am convinced that his entire system is based on false assumptions. Not only does he profess to construct a synthesis from an analytical premise, but he takes his insanity even further, basing his conclusions exclusively on his own practical experience, and passing off the results as if they were absolute truths. Of course, his precepts do also include some legitimate insights and other accurate observations; these, however, come from other masters, whom he has plagiarized, though I can't say to what extent he did so consciously. The idea of the struggle for the center—which Nimzowitsch appropriates—was actually enunciated by Paul Morphy more than a century ago, and taken up by Chigorin and by Pillsbury himself. And what about Nimzowitsch's self-evident truism that it is good to occupy the seventh rank, or that it is better to exploit two of the opponent's weaknesses rather than one? It is with these and similar banalities that Nimzowitsch managed to make a name for himself in England and in New York—not in America, by God, because the Jewish city of New York is by no means synonymous with America. Nimzowitsch himself was barely able to put these theories of his into practice. When I defeated him in Bled, in 1931, in just nineteen moves, he went around whining and telling everyone that I had been disrespectful, treating him as if he were the lowest of the patzers. What was I supposed to do? Let him go ahead and demonstrate his weird notions just to please him? Whatever became of his theories on 'Super Protection,' and about waiting for one's opponent to make a mistake?"

"Dr. Alekhine, doesn't it, then, seem like rather a bitter twist of fate that your next opponent is Russian by birth, Soviet by adoption, an ardent communist, and Jewish to boot?" Correira asks, returning to the interrogation.

"You do well to remind me. It is indeed this last 'quality' of his that shows how right I am. Of the trio of possible challengers, including the Austrian Eliskases and the Estonian Keres, both Aryans, it is no surprise that the choice fell on Botvinnik."

"Is there a danger, therefore, that the title might fall into the hands of Soviet Jews?"

"Over my dead body," Alekhine responds, with a contemptuous smile.

■

MEANWHILE, THE SARABAND of the waiters has resumed: other unusual seafood delicacies appear in sequence, while for Alekhine, the chef himself, working over the rainbow flame of a Bunsen burner, finalizes the preparation of his much-extolled filet of beef Stroganoff.

But Correira has another question in store for him: "Dr. Alekhine, we've heard you rail against the Soviets, against the Jews, but so far you have not treated us to a single word of censure for the Nazis. Yet you must certainly be aware that at this time a trial against them is taking place in Nuremberg, a trial that is unparalleled in human history."

There, the game has reached its climax: his opponent is about to unleash the final attack. "Any words of censure from me would have as much effect as adding a drop of water to the ocean," Alekhine pronounces.

"Or perhaps you don't wish to bite the hand that has fed you up till now?"

"I don't understand what you are alluding to."

"You received a monthly salary of eight hundred marks from the Reich, as *Fachberater für Ostfragen*, consultant for Eastern affairs."

Hearing these words, he has the strange sensation of splitting in two: he, Alexandre Alekhine, finds himself observing an automaton, as though from a distance—his double, who is trying to express properly a tortuous, tentacular thought that has tormented him for years. Back when he worked for the criminal police, he had learned to recognize and neutralize all the defensive techniques employed by his suspects, but now he himself is on the stand, and he can't help making use of the same ploys.

Deny, always deny, even in the face of the most glaring evidence.

"That's not true—I have never received anything from the German government beyond a ration card and awards for my victories in various tournaments. I never had anything to do with it or with its representatives. I played chess for Nazi Germany only because that was the only way to stay alive, and it was also the price of guaranteeing my wife's freedom—she, as you must know, was considered a *Halbjude*, half Jewish. Looking back at the facts and at the situation I was in at the time, I can only say that I would act the same way now. And, regarding my alleged role as a collaborator, I have nothing to add. Those years destroyed me, physically and spiritually, and I am, frankly, somewhat amazed to find that I am still able to play chess. As for the articles that have been attributed to me, I had to remain silent about them for a long time, for fear of reprisals, but as soon as the Allies liberated Paris, I clarified my position at the first opportunity, in several interviews, in an attempt to present the facts in their proper perspective. And I believe I have by now adequately explained that there was nothing of mine in those articles published in 1941 in the *Pariser Zeitung*!"

"You will not deny, however, that you have counted a few prominent Nazis among your friends, Dr. Alekhine—isn't that so?"

Only then does he notice that Correira has a voluminous file open beside his plate. Where did that come from? He is certain that it concerns him. But was it there from the beginning of the meal, or did he only produce it now? Slowly but surely the banquet has become an actual trial. How can that be? When had a defendant's entrance into a courtroom ever been greeted so warmly? When had a prosecutor ever eulogized a defendant so glowingly before proceeding to indict him?

"Must I repeat the question, Dr. Alekhine? Or should I call you *Herr* Alekhine?"

He does not answer, just continues to stare at the dish in front of him. The meat has a rubbery appearance, it looks inedible; its yellowish sauce is veined with red, like the sclera of a bloodshot eye. Alekhine has the vague suspicion that they've served him boiled sea monster, drowned in its own pus. He can barely keep himself from retching. He pushes the plate away, preferring to cleanse his palate with another glass of Aragonês. Its color also calls blood to mind—freshly spilled blood. The taste is intoxicating, but does its bitter aftertaste perhaps stem from a vine fertilized by the putrefaction of a dog? "A good way to deal with the carcasses," Correira had said when they first met at dinner, as he poured that same wine. Alekhine wonders why he should go on sitting at the table, enduring that insane invective. What's keeping him there? His impulse is to leave, but he is convinced that the door is guarded by a robust waiter ready to bar the way.

His inquisitor, meanwhile, opens the file and takes out several photographs that are passed around by the guests. One shows Alekhine at first board with a flag bearing the insignia of the Reich beside him; another shows him with Hans Frank, intently discussing a game; and, finally, there's a group photo, in which the Reichsminister is sitting between Alekhine and his wife, Grace.

The passing around of those images—from which he looks away—seems to prompt a current of mutual consent among the guests: by common accord, they assume expressions ranging from shock to outrage, which remain stamped on their faces, as in a *tableau vivant*. It seems to Alekhine that the jurors are about to reach a unanimous decision. Correira waits patiently until the photographs have made their way around the table, and replaces them in the file with a flourish before renewing his attack.

"We know, Dr. Alekhine, that you had a long association with Hans Frank, now charged with crimes against humanity. Tell us, was Dr. Frank kind to you? He often hosted you at his home, isn't that so? First in Germany, then in Poland. We also know that he made his personal tailor available to you, and even his dentist, who, perhaps using gold extracted from the mouth of a Jew, restored all the teeth you lost in Buenos Aires. Tell us what he was like in private, that refined torturer, that patron of the art of chess . . . Was he generous with you? Between games, did he also take you to watch the slaughter?"

Pretend not to understand the gravity of the accusation. Consent from time to time to some admission of venial facts.

"I associated with Hans Frank, I admit, but only because of chess. He was a true devotee of our game. He had an enormous library of chess books, the likes of which I had never seen before. For him it was a great privilege to be my host. But I never had any feelings of friendship for him."

"And tell us, Dr. Alekhine, did you never hear anything about the other activities of your patron?"

Answer a question with a question.

"Which activities?"

"I will reformulate the question: Did you ever hear anything about the systematic extermination being carried out by your friend? Did you ever hear of Treblinka, Sobibór, Majdanek, Auschwitz . . . ?"

Continue to deny everything, but let a partial truth reinforce the lie.

"I never suspected anything, and if some word of it ever reached me, I always refused to believe it. Hans Frank had high-minded, artistic, humanitarian interests. He himself was an artist; he loved art in all its expressions. He studied in Rome, had spent a long time in Italy, and was a great admirer of Italian painting. He loved music— Schumann, Chopin, Liszt—which he performed with great skill at the piano. He liked to assume the pose of a Renaissance prince surrounded by his court—but he also had to submit to the orders of his superiors, with whom he was often at odds. I was completely unaware of what was happening. I thought there was an overpopulation problem, hence the need to relocate large masses of people. Once, I heard him shout on the phone, 'There are too many of them, and the transport is inadequate. We were supposed to move three thousand, and we only loaded six hundred.'"

"Didn't you ever notice the way Jews were treated? Not even during your stay in Poland? Come, now, Dr. Alekhine, you cannot expect us to believe that an intelligent, sensitive man like you never suspected anything. Or maybe, since they were Jews, after all, you didn't really mind the thought of getting rid of a certain number of them, since that could only help ensure the Aryan purity of your game?"

Assume an attitude of naïve innocence.

"As I have said, I was not thinking of anything but playing chess. And I do not believe I have ever hurt anyone by doing so."

A lengthy silence follows. Particles suspended in a liquid, slowly settling to the bottom. Alekhine begins to wonder if he might be dreaming. He searches for some detail that would confirm it. When entering a hotel room for the first time, he has always had a superstitious need to find, among the elaborate floral designs covering the walls, the seams in the wallpaper: once you find one, all the others leap out at you. Similarly, all he needs is to find one small discrepancy here in order to dismantle the entire complex appearance of a dream. What does he expect to find? A hand with six fingers? A goat's hoof sticking out from under the tablecloth? The face of a dead man? But he can find nothing unusual in his accusers. The only anomaly he finds is in Senhor Correira's voice, which, no longer querulous, has become increasingly cavernous—as if it were no longer coming from out of that vicious little man, but was in Alekhine's own head.

■

"ONE LAST QUESTION, Dr. Alekhine," the voice intones. "Did you ever save the life of a Jew?"

"The situation never arose."

"Really? Yet Sämisch, whom you know well, and who surely doesn't have even a drop of Semitic blood in his veins, has stated that, thanks to your close friendship with Frank, you could have asked him to grant a pardon to the Polish champion Dawid Przepiórka, guilty only of having set foot in *Juden verboten* premises to watch a chess tournament, and for that condemned to death."

React to the accusations with righteous indignation.

"Sämisch is lying! He, and so many others who claimed to be my friends, were only biding their time, waiting around in hopes of seeing me go under. Since there was no way to trounce me on the board, they had to fall back on other methods, among them slander. The truth is that I only learned about Przepiórka's death sentence a year after the fact. And it was precisely as a result of my harsh criticisms of Frank that our relations became strained, before being broken off altogether. The Jews weren't enough, the Bolsheviks weren't enough . . . After the war ended, everyone started vying to see who could smear the most mud on me, hoping to bury me. I have often lied over the years, I don't deny it. Sometimes I did it purely for fun, sometimes out of necessity, but I want you to know one thing: everything that I have told you today is true."

And with those words, Alekhine at last stands up; he feels the time has come to deliver his closing argument in his own defense. Before he begins, he pauses briefly and observes the faces of his accusers one by one. They are all motionless, stony in their expressions of contempt.

"Ladies and gentlemen, I am certainly no saint—indeed, some have called me a real bastard, and I have done a number of things I regret. I never offered much affection either to my wives or to my children, and perhaps I never found time to cultivate even a single true friendship in my life. I have loved only my mother and chess, and it was to chess that I dedicated myself entirely, since early childhood. The chessboard has been my means of artistic expression: the canvas on which I have painted, my musician's staff, the blank page for my poetry. My devotion to it has been such that I have been compelled to play even in the most abject conditions. While bedridden due to illness, I kept myself alive by re-creating entire games in my mind. I have played in the darkness of a cell, I have played while hungry and cold, among the living dead, when the urgent rumblings of our empty stomachs greatly hindered our concentration. I even played on the eve of being sent before a firing squad. Chess has been the star that guided me through my rare periods of calm as well as through the most terrifying storms—through every one of life's difficult moments. Without it, I could not have survived. I have practiced this rigorous, challenging art in complete solitude, and with uncertain financial prospects—it's a well-known fact that the arts were designed by a divinity completely devoid of practical sense. I have devoted an entire lifetime to the pursuit of artistic perfection, I have created works whose profundity few people in the world can fully appreciate, and at times I came so close to reaching the summit of Olympus that I was able to reach out and touch the gods.

"That is all I can say in my defense. If I must pay for what I've done, here I stand, ready."

His words were greeted by silence. They all continued sitting there, frozen. Only Senhora Correira, staring straight into his eyes, moved—once again running her index finger across her throat.

◾

ONE OF ALEKHINE'S most distressing nightmares has always been finding himself trapped in some enclosed space—a cell, a dungeon, a morgue—surrounded by windowless walls: a situation from which, despite every effort, he cannot escape. Making it to the door, turning the knob, and firmly pushing it open: that's the only salvation. But getting there is not easy, because his legs go limp and his feet seem to be stuck to the floor, like metal-plated shoes on a magnet.

That is how he feels now: trapped. The faces of those present seem to lose their contours and gradually melt, like the wax dripping onto the silver candelabras. Alekhine raises his glass for one last, mocking, solitary toast. After emptying it in one gulp, and with a huge effort of will, he staggers toward the door. He has no idea what awaits him out there. The only certainty left to him is that of being able to keep his title until his death.

XIX.

H E OPENED HIS eyes and found himself huddled in his usual armchair, oppressed by mortal dread. The wind, like a mad pianist, was
performing an insistent glissando over the shutters. His chessboard
sat in front of him, the pieces stranded in the same position as always.
His heart was pounding in his chest, his hands were trembling, and
there was a bad taste in his mouth. He felt as though he had awakened from a nightmare that he would rather not remember, though
the echo of its terror persisted. All that remained of it was its after-
effect, an aching feeling of emptiness. But, even now, he wasn't at all
certain of being awake. Indeed, for a moment the thought crossed his
mind that he might have escaped from one nightmare into another,

from which he would never awaken. Panic-stricken, he leaped up and headed frantically for the door. But nothing had changed: there was the usual view of the corridor, dimly lit by sparse wall lamps. He glanced at his wristwatch; it had stopped at ten. He remembered that, just as he was about to change his clothes, a sudden idea had sent him back to the chessboard. But what had happened after that?

He lingered in front of the mirror for some time, then went to the wardrobe and looked through the clothes hanging there. He had always thought that people's apparel not only distinguishes them by wealth, profession, and standing, but also has the power to intimidate their detractors and enemies. If, instead of dressing like a plebeian, the last king of France had held to his rank, wearing royal raiment, perhaps no one would have dared harm a hair on his head. Even in chess, the figure of the King is untouchable, and at that moment he, Aleksandr Aleksandrovich Alekhin, was King. He had to remain seated on his throne, crown on his head and scepter clasped tightly in his fist. It was therefore of great importance that he take extreme care with his attire.

·

HE HAD NO idea what time it was, but it mattered little. As he went down the stairs, he thought it unusual that the music had already stopped in the ballroom—generally, it went on until after midnight. All he could hear were the cries of people leaving, their voices raised in a few timid protests. Who knows? Perhaps there had been a raid by the political police. No reason to be surprised; the men of the PIDE might order the sudden evacuation of any premises at any time. The dining room was empty. And the dance floor as well: a double bass lying on its side and a saxophone leaning against a chair seemed almost abandoned on the stage where the band had been playing.

An eerie silence hung all around; the only sign of life came from an adjoining room. The door was continually opening to let waiters through, their carts laden with delicacies. Inside, Alekhine caught a glimpse of people sitting around a large table, illuminated by dozens of candelabras. That was where they were waiting for him, to celebrate. He took a few steps forward to see better, but as he got closer, a sense of impending menace drove him back. He wondered if his double was in there, even now being forced to undergo a merciless interrogation. Then he turned away and, crossing the now deserted lobby, left the hotel.

As soon as he stepped outside, a gust of wind struck him, taking his breath away. The date palms quivered like gigantic elytra, and, all around, the stand of maritime pines materialized like a procession of flagellants. Despite the approaching storm, Alekhine went down the stairs leading to the beach. It was the first time he had ever taken that path at night. The lighthouse's beacon winked in the distance; the frothing waves crashed against the rocks. In the flashes of lightning, he saw the shades of slaughtered petrels plunge into a purple sea . . .

THE FINAL SECRET

I WAS ABOUT TO leave Portugal at this point, though my search had not produced the desired result. Without a satisfactory conclusion, my novel was doomed to be rewritten from the ground up, or might even end up in the trash. But fortune came to my aid: when I returned from walking the stretch of rugged coastline leading to the lighthouse one last time—the seafront I now called "Promenade Alekhine"—I was approached by a woman who said she was an employee at the Hotel do Parque.

"My name is Violeta da Silva," she began without preamble. "I heard from a friend who works at the hotel where you are staying that you are interested in talking to someone who knew Dr. Alexandre Alekhine personally."

My eyes widened; I didn't say a word, but my expression must have been quite eloquent, because she went on: "As a young man, my father worked as a waiter at the Hotel do Parque, and was assigned to serve him his meals in his room."

The woman left me the address of the place where I could find her father after a certain hour: a tavern in Lisboa Antigua. The old town, uphill, could be reached on foot or by taking a small tram. The pub was frequented mostly by locals, too far off the beaten track for tourists. Indoors, it was stifling, but on the back patio you could enjoy a little cool air. If my calculations were correct, the person I was looking for had to be slightly over eighty. I had no trouble recognizing him: lean and lanky, with a goatee, and long white hair tied back in a ponytail, Manuel da Silva was sitting at a table by himself with a chessboard in front of him, already set up; it looked as though he were waiting for someone.

I went over to him. "Senhor da Silva?"

He looked up and stared at me awhile from behind a pair of thick-lensed glasses.

Then he invited me to sit down. He didn't look at all annoyed by my sudden intrusion: more curious than put out. He offered me a drink. I politely refused, and sat on the edge of my chair, ready to get up if anyone came. As soon as I mentioned Alekhine's name, da Silva's eyes flashed.

"*O imortal!*" he exclaimed.

But he wasn't able to continue, because at that moment his friend arrived, and I stood up to let him have my seat. Completely ignoring me, the newcomer—an elderly, rather stout man—sat down at once, like a walrus settling onto his favorite rock.

"It would be nice to talk about Alekhine, but this isn't a good time," da Silva said, throwing a meaningful look at his gruff friend. "Come and see me tomorrow, around five o'clock. I live not far from here . . ." He scribbled his address on a paper napkin for me, then turned his attention to the game.

THE HOUSE WAS distinguished from others by its late Gothic architecture, with towers, mullioned windows, and griffins at the corners of its eaves. The stone walls were locked in the embrace of a wisteria vine that climbed to the second row of windows, coiling round the slender spiral columns of the terrace.

At five o'clock on the dot, I rang the doorbell. The door was opened by a woman in her fifties, youthful, petite, with Asian features, who, after bowing slightly, invited me in and led me to what had to be the living room, telling me that her husband would join me right away. The room was sunk in shadow. I had the opportunity to look around. The walls, where they were not lined with books, were covered with photographs depicting da Silva at various ages. From what I could see, he must have traveled a lot.

"I was a war correspondent for fifty years."

I started. I hadn't heard him come in. Leaning on a cane, da Silva walked over to the balcony and opened the shutters to let in the afternoon light.

"Fifty years of wars all over the planet. My second wife, whom you just met, was still a child when I took her out of Saigon, rescuing her from the bombing."

He invited me to sit in an old armchair whose leather was crisscrossed by a dense network of crinkles. He himself took a chair that looked rather uncomfortable, but forced him to hold his torso upright. He seemed to have a back problem.

"So—you're thinking of writing a novel about Alekhine's death."

"Actually, I've already written it, but I don't have an ending, and I'm hoping you can help me find one."

Da Silva smiled.

"In a novel you can say things that in other contexts would

165

be forbidden. Then again, perhaps only the imagination allows us to arrive at certain hidden truths. In my profession as a correspondent, I always adhered to reality. I, too, wanted to write something about those distant events—I collected quite a lot of material on the subject—but then I gave it up. I would only have ended up saying what others had said before me. But you intend to write a novel, and that guarantees you a certain privilege."

I could not help being struck by this paradoxical statement. I took a miniature recorder out of my pocket, but he waved his hand, gesturing for me to put it away. Pointing a finger to his head, he told me that it was better to leave everything stored in the memory, and let it develop there over time. Only afterward would I be able to write.

■

"FOR THE ENTIRE duration of the war," he began, "Estoril was a free port: Allies, Nazis, and secret agents of various nationalities shared it equitably, stimulating local commerce. Then, suddenly, with the advent of peace, the hotels emptied out, and numerous shops closed, one after another. My father, like many others, owned a fishing boat, but by then, more often than not, what he caught remained unsold. So my parents decided to send me to work at the Hotel do Parque. I was fifteen, and I was the third of five brothers. I would be provided with board and lodging and the opportunity to learn a trade. I would not earn a penny, no, but at least there would be one less mouth at home to feed. At most I could count on customers' tips—and although the bathing season didn't start until May, by the end of March there was usually a certain trickle of tourists to be counted on. There was nearly a full staff, except for waiters. I did a little of everything: I helped make up the rooms, polished the silverware, even gave the gardener a hand. And among my various duties was that of serving meals to the room of the only guest then staying at the hotel.

"The first few times I went in with the food trolley, my legs were shaking. The other members of the staff liked to scare me. When we gathered for meals, they enjoyed themselves at my expense, telling me to be careful with Alekhine, because the last boy who used to serve his meals—a boy my own age—had disappeared without a trace . . .

"The truth is, Alekhine wasn't particularly forbidding. On the contrary, he treated me with brisk kindness—but he was certainly a man of few words. I was amazed to find that he spoke Portuguese so well."

"MY BUNK WAS in a large space used as a storeroom, located behind the kitchen. I was given a kind of loft, so close to the ceiling that I had to be careful not to bump my head when I got up. This ceiling, in fact, was located just below Room 43, so at night I heard Alekhine's footsteps—pacing back and forth for hours. Once, I sneaked out of my sleeping quarters and went up to his floor, going as far as the door to his room. For a while, there was silence; then I heard something that made my hair stand on end: a muffled moan, like the whimper of a wounded beast. I ran away as fast as I could, and that moan echoed in my ears until dawn, preventing me from falling asleep. The next morning, I hesitated a moment before knocking. Who knows what I was actually afraid of? But when I entered, everything was in order, and Alekhine, as usual, was in his armchair, in front of his chessboard."

Da Silva seemed to be sifting through his memories.

"At times, he was so focused on the game that he didn't notice my presence. One day, I lingered to watch him: I couldn't understand what he found so interesting about those pieces of wood. Suddenly, he looked up and asked me if I knew how to play. I said yes, but as I told that lie, my cheeks turned fiery red. 'Come, I'll teach you,' he said, to my great surprise. He didn't really teach me anything, however. He merely showed me the bizarre movement of the Knight. Still, that was enough to intrigue me, enough so that subsequently I was determined to learn the game on my own. I did not become a great player—the life I led did not permit me to apply myself as I would have liked—but today I am still one of the few players in the world, perhaps the only one, able to say that the person who introduced me to the Knight's move was the great Alekhine."

■

"HOW DID HE spend his days?" I asked. "I have tried to imagine it, but I'd like to hear it from you . . ."

"He devoted much of his time to chess. He was all alone in that big hotel, deserted in the winter season. He took walks along the beach. Since it was rumored that he was a Nazi, sometimes, as I watched him walking along the shoreline, I expected a U-boat to emerge from the water at any moment, sent from Germany to pick him up. Another interest of his was reading—he loved detective stories, authors like Wallace, Chandler, Ellery Queen . . . The last book he was reading, however, was not a mystery novel, but a love story between a Nazi and a Jewish woman: *Chosen Races*, by Margaret Sothern."

"As far as I know," I said, "Alekhine did not have much sympathy for the Jews."

"In my opinion, Alekhine was not a racist. This is demonstrated by the fact that in his final days he became friends with a Jew. He embodied instead a form of extreme class-consciousness, inspired by the very lofty concept that he held for art in general, and for chess in particular. Alekhine represented an unparalleled model for all the masters of the time: his game, his insights, eluded the comprehension of even the leading experts. Unlike Capablanca, he loved the most complex positions: where chaos reigned for others, he moved at his ease, like a tiger in a canebrake. The common man, however, tends to gloss over the sublime qualities of an artist, and judges the individual based on the image, often distorted, that the media present him with. The press continued to describe Alekhine as a monster, a drunkard, a fortune hunter, a traitor to his own country, a friend of one of the most heinous Nazi criminals. Who would take the trouble to speak out in favor of such a man? Speaking of which, I believe that his long association with Hans Frank can also be explained by the great love Alekhine had for chess. In his eyes, the governor of Poland was a prince, a patron of the art of chess, and a fervent enthusiast in his own right. Moreover, he was capable of guaranteeing Alekhine the material security that he was always searching for. And when has an artist ever concerned himself about his benefactor's political choices?"

After rummaging through a drawer crammed with papers, da Silva showed me a photograph depicting Alekhine with his wife, Grace, who was holding a cat in her arms, surrounded by a group of people. The snapshot, faded by now, had been taken in the winter of '41 at a harbor in Estoril.

"These people you see," he said, "were all in some way related to the secret police, who spied on but also protected him. Alekhine loved our country, and for Portugal it was a great honor to host the world chess champion. His stay at the Hotel do Parque was fully paid for out of government funds."

"One must therefore rule out the possibility that the PIDE had anything to do with his death . . ."

"I wouldn't say that. On the contrary. Although Portugal had declared itself neutral, over the course of the conflict it showed clear Nazi sympathies. The German regime deposited considerable tons of gold in the country's coffers, which, after the war, no one claimed possession of. But after the defeat of the Third Reich, things changed. New political alliances were in sight, new economic interests. Portugal had to make the world forget its pro-Nazi leanings. Faced with such issues, I couldn't say how much a man's life might still have been worth."

I was itching to talk about Alekhine's death, but for da Silva time followed much more expansive trajectories than it did for me. He went on showing me photos of people of that era, pausing each time to tell me their life stories, with as much pride as someone sharing a family album.

■

"WERE YOU THE first to find him dead?" I finally asked.

"So they wanted people to believe. That night, I was awakened by loud noises coming from the room above—not the usual measured pacing, to which by then I had become accustomed, but the sort of scurrying about that could only be caused by several people. For a while, I lay there listening, but, ultimately, I couldn't resist the temptation to go see what was happening. I left my room, ran up the stairs, and peered cautiously into the corridor. The door of Alekhine's room was open, the lights were on, and there was agitated whispering coming from inside. Suddenly, a man stepped out and stared in my direction. Had he seen me? I thought I should get away as quickly as possible, but when I reached the first landing, I heard someone else coming up the stairs from below. All I could do was crouch behind a large ornamental plant, closing my eyes and praying that the Madonna would make me invisible. Some people stumbled past me, swearing under their breath. At first, I assumed they were drunks. Only when I imagined they must have reached the next floor and were about to step into the corridor did I peek out and see two men struggling to carry a big bundle wrapped in a tarpaulin. It didn't even occur to me that Alekhine's body might be in there.

"The next morning, I was summoned by the manager, who told

me that the master had given him orders not to be disturbed by anyone before eleven o'clock. This struck me as rather unusual, since Alekhine was a creature of habit: for weeks, I'd been instructed to serve him his breakfast every day at exactly nine o'clock. And I was all the more eager to go up to his room so I could tell him that a telegram had just arrived from London. When I went in, I saw him sitting in the armchair. He appeared to be sleeping. I had found him dozing before, but usually he woke up as soon as he heard the door open. I immediately thought it was strange that he was wearing a coat (which, incidentally, I had never seen) instead of his usual smoking jacket, and that there were empty dishes scattered on the table in front of him. The night before, in fact, I had not served him dinner, since the management had arranged a banquet in his honor, in a private room downstairs. I called him several times, but he didn't move. I stepped closer, and only then did I see a trickle of caked drool at the corner of his mouth. I touched his arm, which was as rigid as wood. I was paralyzed with fear, but even before I could recover and alert anyone, the room had filled with people anyway. I had the distinct impression that the police had already been at the hotel for some time and were only waiting for a signal to enter the scene. News of Alekhine's death spread like wildfire, and in less than an hour the lobby was jammed with curious onlookers and journalists. Among them was the Jewish violinist with whom Alekhine had become friends. He was weeping—he couldn't get over it. The irony of fate! Abandoned by all, with only a Jew left to mourn him.

"Alekhine's body was taken away that same morning. The furniture and his personal effects were also cleared out and moved elsewhere. The door was locked, and even the room's number plate was removed."

"Why the rush?"

"They had to keep the curious away, especially journalists. There was an official story that had to be protected. And the autopsy report served the same purpose."

"But why was there talk of asphyxia?"

"Alekhine spent numerous hours glued to the chessboard, and so as not to get distracted he ate his meals—for the most part meat—by occasionally fishing a bite off his plate with his fingers, as if he were nibbling cookies. This kept him from having to turn his attention away from the game. So Dr. d'Aguiar, having learned of this particular habit, seized the opportunity to attribute the cause of death to something that fell within his area of expertise."

"What do you mean by that?"

"Dr. d'Aguiar was an authority in the field of forensic traumatology, and was known for having written a long treatise on the causes and symptoms of suffocation. Consequently, his diagnosis was unlikely to be questioned."

"It was a false statement, then?"

Before replying, da Silva allowed himself a brief pause.

"Only when Salazar's power began to weaken, when there was no longer much danger that every individual one met was in fact a member of the secret police, only then did Dr. Antonio Jacinto Ferreira, who had countersigned the autopsy results, decide to reveal, albeit confidentially, the truth about Alekhine's death. The doctor was an ardent amateur chess player, and we frequented the same club, though you could not exactly say that we were friends. I knew that he, too, had been involved in the regime's activities, and that did not make me particularly well disposed toward him.

"One night, around midnight, I went into a small Lisbon café for a drink. There was no one at the bar, and the owner was just waiting for his four last customers—all sitting around the same table—to ask for their bill, so he could close. One of the four was Dr. Ferreira. Unintentionally, I'd sat down in a corner from which I could hear every word of what they were saying. I was tempted to change seats, but as I was about to do so, I realized that the topic was Alekhine's death. The person speaking was Ferreira himself. And he was telling them that on that long-ago evening, the night before his death, Alekhine had not shown up at the banquet arranged in his honor. After the guests had waited for him for over an hour, a waiter had been instructed to go and summon him, but, despite repeated knocks at his door, he hadn't answered. Around eleven o'clock, there was a 'peaceful' raid by the political police, which caused the ballroom to clear out. People were urged to leave, and the hotel guests were asked to return to their rooms. Perhaps because of the presence of a high-ranking prelate, the banquet participants, gathered in a private room, were accorded special treatment and allowed to finish their dinner undisturbed. The night porter, who had just started working there, would later say that he had seen Alekhine go out right after curfew, just as a storm was about to break.

"And this is where our Dr. Ferreira came in. From what he was saying, at seven o'clock the following morning he was awakened by a phone call from the Hotel do Parque: it was Luís Lupi, informing him of Alekhine's death and asking Ferreira to join him as soon as possible. When he arrived at the scene, Ferreira also found Dr. d'Aguiar there. Alekhine's body, wrapped in a sheet, had been laid out on the floor of his room. Ferreira said that all it took was a quick glance to see that the death was due to a gunshot wound to the heart. At that point, Luís Lupi had taken him aside, along with Dr. d'Aguiar . . .

"I couldn't hear what followed, because the owner had started lowering the shutter. I tried to slip out before the four of them, but it's certain Ferreira saw me, because from then on his attitude toward me changed drastically—he did everything he could to avoid me, and eventually even started ignoring me entirely. Although I did not hear the end of his story that night, it seems clear to me that Ferreira, Lupi, and d'Aguiar had been agreeing on an official version to convey to the press."

"Then Dr. Ferreira was also part of the PIDE?"

Da Silva smiled.

"So they said. In any case, at that time, bowing to the dictates of the regime meant being complicitous regardless. Those who refused either rotted in prison or were simply eliminated. Then there was an actual official hierarchy, of which Luís Lupi was undoubtedly part: he was a leading exponent of the Sociedade de Propaganda de Portugal, which was essentially the official face of the PIDE."

"So—the secret police were absolutely involved in Alekhine's death!"

"Of course. Although I don't believe anyone could say to what extent, precisely. Perhaps they had been ordered from the beginning to assist in the planning phase of a mission that others would later carry out."

"To set the stage for an execution . . ." I murmured thoughtfully. "That's why they had him wear the overcoat! To hide the blood-stains."

Da Silva nodded. "Naturally, Ferreira was forced to corroborate the result of the autopsy, or maybe, who knows, he himself forced d'Aguiar to add his own signature—we'll never know. The fact is that, twenty years later, writing to Alekhine's son, Ferreira once again reiterated that the death was due to asphyxia, adding that there were no grounds to justify the possibility of suicide or murder. Still, it is my belief that, if he subsequently felt the need to relate an incident that certainly does him no honor from an ethical standpoint, he most likely was telling the truth . . ."

"But, in that case, who were the masterminds behind it?"

Da Silva paused again before replying. "There are two hypotheses. The first is that it was the French: it was open season throughout

Europe on anyone who had collaborated with Vichy. The second possibility, which in my view is more plausible, is that the order came from the Kremlin. It hardly seems like such an improbable hypothesis when one remembers that, a few years after his father's death, Alekhine's son himself stated publicly that 'the hand of Moscow reached my father' . . ."

"But why?"

"To me it seems quite clear: with Alekhine dead, the title would remain vacant."

I still did not understand. "Were they perhaps afraid that Alekhine might win the match?"

"Alekhine was considered a genius at chess, and anything can be expected of a genius. There was therefore the possibility, albeit remote, that he might retain the title. A victory on his part would have been an intolerable blow to the Soviet Union. What's more, Alekhine still appeared to be in good health—no one could have suspected that he was so seriously ill, and that his body would not have been able to sustain the stress.

"But that was just one of their fears, the least of them. By then, the harbingers of what in the coming decades would be called the Cold War were already looming. And if the weapons of the two blocs were to remain unused, it was essential that there be other arenas in which they could compete and excel. Chess was therefore, as ever, a symbolic substitute for war: gaining supremacy in it was a constant reminder to the enemy that you possessed greater military expertise, a more effective strategy. With Alekhine still alive, however, there was the danger that someone might put pressure on the members of the federation to force him to abdicate because of his pro-Nazi past. In that case, the title would technically have returned to Max Euwe. And according to the regulations, the Dutch champion had the option of choosing another opponent—instead of confronting Botvinnik, he could have accepted the challenge of the United States'

Reshevsky. If the latter were to win, the world crown would have been delivered into the hands of the reviled Americans. With Alekhine's death, on the other hand, the title remained vacant, and to designate a new champion it would be necessary to organize a knockout elimination tournament among the world's strongest players, all of whom were Soviet. Their victory was therefore assured. Alekhine's death, in fact, solved everything."

Da Silva seemed worn out by our long conversation. He ran a hand over his hair. His fingers were long and pale, the skin so delicate as to appear bluish. Just then, his wife came in, announcing the arrival of his physiotherapist.

"I hope I was of help to you," he said, rising from his chair with some effort. "Unfortunately, however, I must now leave you. My back requires treatment."

I had the distinct feeling that he wanted to add something more, but I hastened to take my leave, thanking him for the time he had afforded me.

■

THERE WAS NOTHING further for me to do in Lisbon: I had obtained more than I'd hoped for. With the information da Silva had given me, I would be able to write an ending to my novel. I therefore prepared to leave. But the day after my visit to da Silva, news of the death of Rui Nascimento appeared in all the local newspapers. I therefore decided to postpone my departure. I, too, attended the funeral service: a solemn, lavish affair. The hearse, drawn by four black horses and followed by a large crowd, stopped at the gates of the cemetery; from there, the coffin was carried to the family crypt on the pallbearers' shoulders.

At the end of the ceremony, as I was walking toward the exit, I noticed da Silva standing at the side of the main walkway. He was with his wife, but as soon as he saw me, he nodded at her to go on alone. He raised his cane in the air to catch my attention.

"Thank you for attending the funeral," he said when I was within hearing distance. "Rui Nascimento was a great man."

Then he took my arm as if for support, though in reality he was leaning close, seemingly about to reveal a secret.

"O último segredo," he said enigmatically.

"Sorry?"

His manner became even more confidential.

"The fact is, I also spoke to Nascimento back when he was thinking of writing a book about Alekhine, before he, too, abandoned the project—perhaps because he had never believed the murder theory, and thought it was all a figment of someone's imagination. Eventually, in 2006, he did go ahead and publish something on Alekhine, which was called O último segredo, in which, however, he avoided touching on the subject of Alekhine's death altogether."

Every so often, he stopped to catch his breath, though actually he was slowing down the pace to have time to finish what he intended to tell me before we reached the gate of the cemetery.

"So what is the final secret?"

Da Silva seemed to be searching for the right words.

"Alekhine's burial took place on April 16 in the cemetery of São João do Estoril. The coffin was lowered into the grave of Manuel Esteva, an obscure Portuguese chess player who never in his life would have imagined deserving such an honor. However, when the remains were exhumed ten years later to be transferred to Montparnasse Cemetery, the undertaker noticed something odd: the femurs of the skeleton were too short to have belonged to a man of Alekhine's stature."

At those words, I had to suppress a shiver.

"So those were not Alekhine's remains?"

Da Silva merely smiled without answering my question. We continued walking toward the exit.

"We can't be certain," he said. "The person who confided this to me was a befuddled old man who, when he took to the bottle, often told such hair-raising stories. Still, I began to wonder why Alekhine had been buried in strict secrecy a whole three weeks after his death. Perhaps because they had to find the cadaver of an anonymous unknown to replace him in the coffin? And, in that case, what had become of his own corpse?

"I was sure that I would never get an answer to that question, but then, fifteen years later, I met a Russian at our club, a Muscovite who was in Lisbon vacationing with his family. At that time, it was a luxury that only a party big shot could afford. He spoke a little French, a language that I, too, know, and we became friendly. All he did was extol the invincibility of the Soviet chess players—little did the poor fellow know that the braggart Bobby Fischer would soon arrive on the scene—and so, one evening, between one game and another, and one drink and another, the talk turned to Alekhine. When I asked him if he had ever visited Alekhine's grave at Montparnasse Cemetery, he looked at me strangely. 'Alekhine is in Moscow, not in Paris,' he replied in an offended tone. I suppressed a laugh. 'What? In Moscow?' I exclaimed. At that point, perhaps realizing that he may have revealed too much, he became evasive. 'His spirit, I mean, his spirit, not his body,' he added quickly, visibly uncomfortable."

■

BY THEN, WE had passed through the gate of the cemetery. A black sedan, a rental car, pulled up to the sidewalk. The driver got out and helped da Silva settle into the backseat, where his wife was already waiting for him. He rolled down the window.

"Imagine," he said, "that Stalin, with the complicity of the Portuguese police, gave the order not only to kill him, but also to bring his body back to his native soil. Although the man was considered a traitor, his genius belonged to Great Mother Russia. Imagine that Alekhine's embalmed body is to this day displayed in a showcase in some secret room in the Kremlin. Imagine that, as the conclusion for your novel."

I saw his eyes twinkle in the car's shadowy interior, a moment before he gave a sign and the vehicle pulled away.

A NOTE ABOUT THE AUTHOR

Paolo Maurensig was born in 1943 in Gorizia, Italy. He worked at numerous jobs—salesman, window dresser, interior designer, and restorer of antique musical instruments, among others—before publishing his first novel at the age of fifty. That novel, *The Lüneburg Variation*, was a bestseller in Italy and an international sensation. He lives in Udine.

A NOTE ABOUT THE TRANSLATOR

Anne Milano Appel has been awarded the Italian Prose in Translation Award (2015), the John Florio Prize (2012), and the Northern California Book Award for Translation—Fiction (2013 and 2014). She has translated works by Claudio Magris, Primo Levi, Andrea Canobbio, Roberto Saviano, and numerous others.